SIGNS AND WONDERS

A WITCHBANE NOVEL #7

MORGAN BRICE

SIGNS AND WONDERS
WITCHBANE BOOK 7

By Morgan Brice

eBook ISBN: 978-1-64795-067-5
Paperback ISBN: 978-1-64795-068-2
Signs and Wonders, Copyright © 2023 by Gail Z. Martin.
Cover by Lou Harper.

Darkwind Press is an imprint of DreamSpinner Communications, LLC

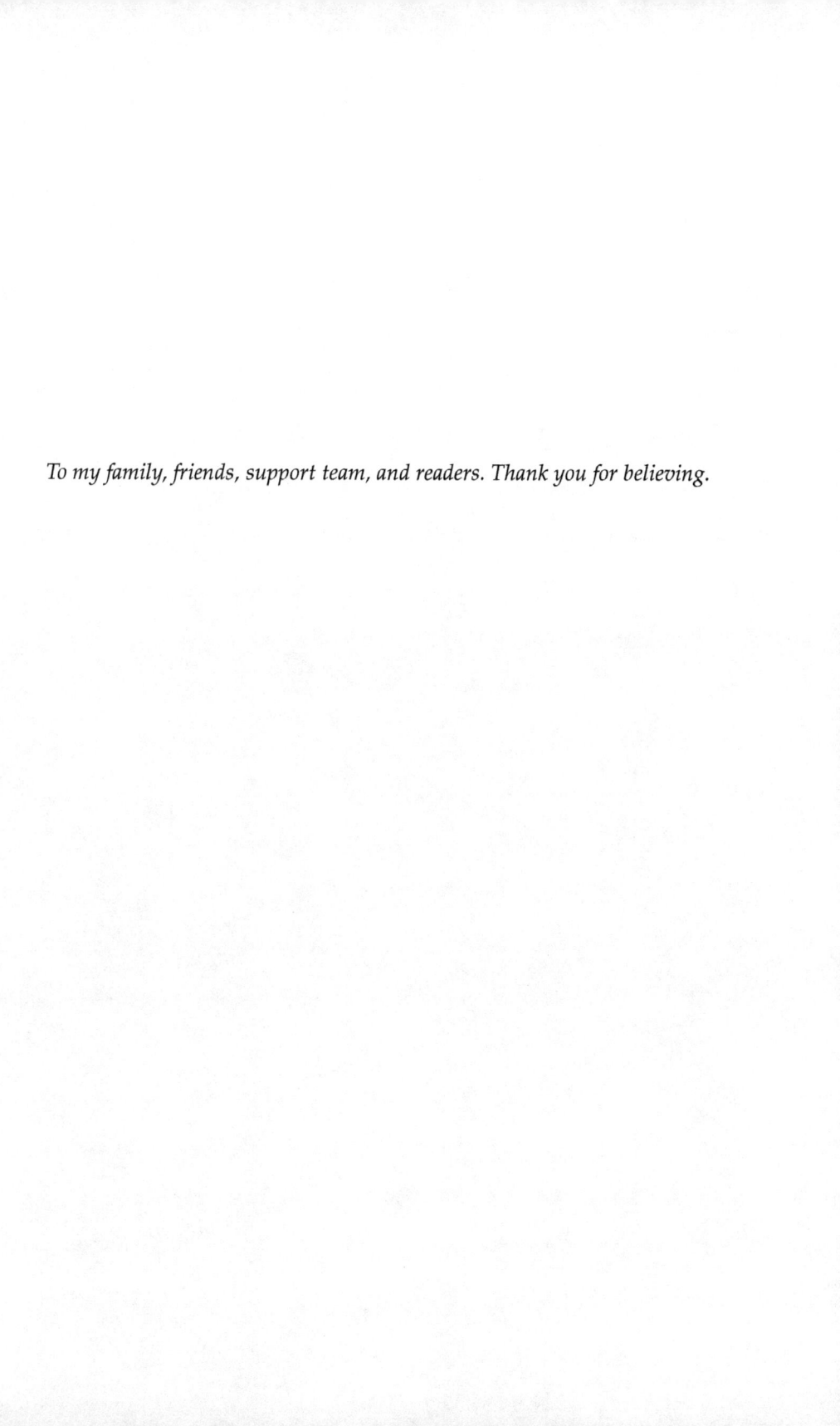

To my family, friends, support team, and readers. Thank you for believing.

1

SETH

"Behind you!" Seth Tanner shouted to alert his partner.

The angry ghost of a woman materialized behind Evan Malone, reaching clawed fingers for his shoulder. Evan dropped to the ground, and Seth's shotgun blast reverberated in the corridor of the abandoned hospital. Rock salt dispelled the ghost and pitted the decaying plaster walls.

Strong, invisible hands seized Seth by one arm and flung him against the wall, knocking the wind out of him. The ghost appeared again and dragged him to his feet. Seth slashed the air with an iron knife, and the ghost shrieked and let go, leaving livid fingerprints behind.

Then the spirit flickered into view in front of Evan, giving him a hard shove toward the broad central stairwell.

"Evan!" Seth knew he couldn't reach his boyfriend fast enough to keep him from falling.

Evan caught the railing with one arm, breaking his fall, and raised the shotgun, firing point-blank at the ghost, who vanished again.

"You okay?" Seth asked, breathless.

Evan warily climbed the few steps he had fallen and reloaded. "I'm not dead. Start the banishment. I've got you covered."

Seth wasn't a witch or a medium, but this particular banishment didn't require that. He chalked symbols carefully onto the tile floor and set down a salt circle to protect Evan and himself while he worked the ritual.

"Jenny Summers, it is time to move on. You may not harm the living, and you can't stay here." Seth spoke the litany from memory. "By all that you hold holy, I beseech you to move on."

"I didn't want to die." The ghost's voice was thick with pain and loss.

"You are dead and buried. This is not your place. Let go and move on to what lies ahead." Seth continued the ritual, although his heart broke for the young woman whose life had been cut short by a thirst for adventure.

"I don't want to go."

Jenny's spirit no longer attacked, weakened by the sigils Seth had chalked. She looked young and scared, lost in a place between life and death.

"Your family and friends cherish your memory. But you do not belong here. Go in peace, and do no more harm. In the name of that which creates, empowers, and sustains, and by the will of all those who loved you—move on."

Jenny's ghost flickered again and then faded as an icy wind swept through the atrium, making dust motes dance in the light.

"Is she gone?" Evan kept his shotgun racked and ready.

"I think so. At least for now, if not permanently. Milo said that if the banishment didn't send her on, it would sap her strength so she couldn't hurt anyone again for a while," Seth replied. "I tried to get one of the local mediums to come with us, but once they found out where we were going, they all said 'hell no.'"

"Guess we were just dumb enough to do it anyhow." Evan's grin made it clear he relished the adventure.

"Sounds like us." Seth bumped Evan's shoulder in agreement.

The abandoned Molly Stark Hospital was legendary for its haunts, but the crazed spirit that attacked them wasn't from the building's past as a tuberculosis sanitarium. Jenny Summers was a much more recent death, an unfortunate urban explorer who had come to investigate the hospital's supernatural reputation and fallen to her death through a hole in the floor.

Unlike the hospital's other ghosts, Jenny's angry spirit lashed out at security guards and tour guides who ventured too near the building. That made her a hazard, meaning someone had to set her soul to rest. When the head of security couldn't persuade any of the local ghost hunters to rid the site of Jenny, he had reached out to Seth's mentor, Milo, who had tapped Seth and Evan since they were passing through the area.

"These old hospitals were built to stand forever, even when no one needed them anymore," Evan noted wistfully as they slipped out the back door, locking it with the key borrowed from the security chief.

The four-story Spanish Revival hospital dated from 1929, when it had been considered cutting-edge in its amenities. Huge windows, wide verandas, and courtyards were meant to provide sunlight and fresh air to patients. By the time it shuttered in the 1990s, medical advances had left the huge complex behind.

"There are over a thousand feet of tunnels running between the main building and the outbuildings," Seth said as they slipped through the cut in the chain link fence. "I'm glad we didn't have to go down there. The ghosts who won't move on might not have been as friendly."

"If you could call Jenny friendly." Evan turned back to look at the hospital, silhouetted against the sky. Even in decay, its archways and columns, the red-tiled roof, and the Mediterranean lines of its design held a faded grandeur.

"No matter how many times we do something like this, I always wonder why the ghosts stick around," Evan mused.

"All the usual reasons. Unfinished business. Fear of the unknown. And while they might not have liked being a patient here, for many of them, it was their last home." Seth mentally wished the spirits well and thanked them for allowing them to come and go in peace.

"Kinda nice to get a simple salt and burn," Evan observed as he limped back to where they parked. "Change of pace. Keeps us in practice."

"Like that was an issue," Seth snarked.

They drove Seth's black pickup back to the campground where they had parked the RV. "Figured we'd take the rest of the day off to recuperate and go on to Pittsburgh tomorrow," Seth said.

"It's still early," Evan remarked.

Seth arched an eyebrow. "And you're limping. I bet your shoulder is killing you." He gave a knowing look at the way Evan held his left arm.

"Nothing some ice won't fix."

"Yeah, well my back hurts from getting body slammed, so indulge me." Seth knew that Evan wouldn't argue about taking the day if it was for Seth's benefit.

"Do we need more supplies?" Evan dropped his argument and eyed Seth with concern.

"I stocked up on Advil and sports cream before we left Cleveland." Seth grimaced as he turned the steering wheel, and his shoulder twinged.

They went through a burger drive-through for lunch and pulled into the campground, tired and aching.

"I really don't feel like setting up the hitch right now." Seth rolled his shoulders and winced as he eyed the connector between the truck and fifth-wheel trailer.

The RV had belonged to Seth's parents, who were planning a grand adventure to celebrate retirement. They died in a car accident before that could happen, leaving the Silverado and RV to Seth.

"Go shower, and I'll set out the first-aid kit." Seth hoped neither of them suffered worse than pulled muscles. "I'll go next, and we can patch each other up. I've got chili in the slow cooker for dinner, so we can take it easy the rest of the day."

"Does that include the healing power of a hand job?" Evan gave him a naughty grin.

"Good endorphins speed recuperation." Seth winked.

Unfortunately, the RV's shower wasn't big enough for both of them. Seth was six foot three, with dirty blond hair, chocolate eyes, and an athletic build. Evan stood just as tall, but built slimmer, with chestnut hair and hazel eyes. Finding a hotel with a shower to accommodate them both was a treat.

Seth made a pot of coffee and set out supplies while Evan showered. He swallowed some ibuprofen and checked the ice packs in the freezer. The image of Evan falling backward toward the staircase flashed on repeat in his memory, and he remembered how his heart froze, thinking he was going to see Evan tumble to his death.

When we finish with the last witch disciple, we're done with this crazy life. We'll get a house with a big shower, maybe in the mountains or at the beach, and we'll stop hunting things that go bump in the night.

Five years ago, Seth came home from the Army happy to be with his family and ready for new beginnings. He and his younger brother Jesse planned a night out making a silly ghost hunting video at a supposedly haunted underpass. Even now, Seth couldn't clearly recall the details of the attack that left him unconscious, but when he woke, he found Jesse's bloody body in the branches of a tree where a sheriff's posse once hanged Rhyfel Gremory, a powerful dark witch.

No one believed Seth's account, and for a time he was suspected of the murder. When he refused to recant his story, he spent months in a mental health facility until he learned to say what they wanted to hear to gain his freedom. While he was there, his parents died and their house burned, leaving him only the truck, the RV, and the Hayabusa motorcycle he had bought when he first returned from the service.

He vowed vengeance on whatever had killed Jesse and sought out anyone who could teach him about the supernatural. That led him to a couple of seasoned monster hunters—Milo and Toby Cornell—who took him in and gave him the knowledge and skills he needed for his quest.

Gremory's coven of a dozen warlocks had sworn vengeance on the sheriff and his posse who killed their master, creating a cycle of ritual murders to punish the deputies' descendants. Seth set out to stop them and fell in love with their next intended victim—Evan.

"There's not much in life that a hot shower doesn't make better." Evan limped into the kitchen. "You made coffee. I love you."

"For my coffee?" Seth teased.

"And other things." Evan pretended to need a few seconds to think. "Your chili's pretty impressive too."

Seth flipped him off as he headed for his shower.

"You're good at that too," Evan joked.

"Later—if you're nice to me."

"Hey! I can be very, very nice," Evan called after him.

Seth let the hot water sluice away sweat and dirt, keeping the spray trained on his sore back. When the hot water ran out, he toweled off and went back to the kitchen, where Evan had put out some snacks.

"Feeling better?" Evan asked.

"Still sore. C'mon—let me have a look at your arm and that leg."

Evan set his coffee aside and unbuttoned his shirt. Seth noticed that he'd avoided a T-shirt, which required more arm movement to get into.

"Can you move through the full range of motion?" Seth was worried.

Evan grimaced, but he rotated his arm in a full circle and then raised and lowered it. "Hurts like a mofo, but it moves."

"All right, let me rub you down, and we'll get some ice on it. Did you take anything?"

"Yep. The pills haven't kicked in yet. And you always rub me the right way." Evan had a mischievous glint in his eyes.

"Trust me—you don't want sports cream in those places." Seth shuddered at the thought. "I learned that lesson the hard way back in middle school."

Evan straddled the chair and stretched out his arm. Seth gently worked the ointment into his skin, starting from the shoulder and moving down his bicep and forearm. He could tell that Evan was doing his best not to react, but from the clench of his jaw, Seth knew it had to hurt.

"I'll do your hip next, then you can put ice on both places," Seth assured him. "Maybe have some whiskey—for medicinal purposes."

"After I do your back," Evan reminded him.

"When we get to Pittsburgh, I want Matt to look at your shoulder." Seth gently massaged the sore muscles. "Just to make sure you haven't fucked up anything in the joint."

"The only thing I want to fuck is you."

"Nice to know. Let's do that when we're not on pain meds," Seth replied. "What's making you limp?"

"I slammed my hip into the marble step when I caught myself," Evan admitted.

Seth wrapped a towel over Evan's bare shoulders and steadied him as he stood to drop his jeans. A dark bruise already spread across his hip. "Yeah, that's gonna hurt for a while," he commiserated, wincing in sympathy.

Evan returned the favor, working the ointment into Seth's sore shoulders and back. When he finished, and they washed their hands thoroughly, Seth retrieved the ice, and they retreated to the couch to re-watch favorite action flicks until supper and let the frozen packs work their magic.

Seth's phone rang halfway through the first movie. "Hey, Milo. Job's done, and we're still mostly in one piece," he greeted his mentor. "You're on speakerphone."

"*Mostly* in one piece?" Milo sounded concerned.

"That ghost had some serious attitude. I can understand why she ran people off," Seth replied. "We sent her on, but we're both going to be black and blue for a while."

"Thanks for taking care of it," Milo said. "Just don't go rushing off to the next witch disciple until you're both back in fighting shape. No sense taking stupid chances."

"We're going to stop in Pittsburgh," Seth told him. "Travis has some new lore from that secret archive he can access, and Brent's heard some fresh info on the witch cartel. And before you ask—I'm going to have Matt check us both over before we head out."

"Damn right you are," Milo agreed. Seth could hear Toby's muffled voice in the distance. "He said they're going to see Travis's medic. Don't make me repeat myself, old man." The fondness in his voice took the sting from his crusty response.

"You hearing anything on the grapevine?" Seth asked Milo.

"Your witch disciple hunt is above the pay grade of most hunters out there," Milo said. "And most of the ones who could handle something like that you've already pulled in. When you get to Buckhannon, get in touch with Drake Carlson. He's FBSI, but don't hold that against him. Drake's one of the good guys, and he can run interference for you if you need it. Tell him he still owes me a bottle of Jack for that card game in Morgantown."

"Will do," Seth promised. "And happy birthday. Got any big plans?"

"Going out for a nice steak dinner and a superhero movie," Milo said. "Figured that stuff like escape rooms and axe throwing was too much like the day job."

"You got our package?" Seth and Evan had sent a boxed Blu-ray set of one of Milo's favorite old TV series, *The Rockford Files*.

"Yeah. Thanks. Great pick. We're already halfway through watching them." Milo cleared his throat. "You two be careful, and keep us posted. You hear me?"

"Loud and clear," Seth replied. He knew Milo's gruff tone hid how much he cared. "Enjoy your day."

He ended the call and wasn't sure how to interpret the expression on Evan's face. "What?"

Evan shrugged. "You ever think we'll be like that?"

"Old and crotchety?"

Evan rolled his eyes. "You know what I mean."

Seth smiled. "Yeah, I do. I hope so. I don't think it was easy for them to step back from going on hunts, but Milo's heart problems made Toby lay down the law. They've got the online security company now, and they're kinda lore masters for the hunting community, plus there's Toby's massive garden."

"Don't forget the dogs and goats," Evan added with a laugh, "now that they're not gone all the time. I think that's how Toby got him to quit. Can't you just hear him? 'If we quit, you can get a dog.'"

Seth chuckled. "You might be right about that. I wouldn't mind that myself when we're done. You ever think about that?"

"All the time," Evan admitted. "You and I can work from anywhere. We could go to the beach in the winter and the mountains in the summer. Maybe get a cabin or something."

Seth worked as a white-hat hacker for Milo and Toby's security company when he wasn't using his skills to hack into the witch disciples' accounts. Evan's passion for photography and his talent for design led to starting his own graphics company and helped with the occasional need to create fake documents for their hunting.

Late in the evening, Evan's phone rang.

"Hi Parker! How's Cleveland?" he greeted his younger brother, making it so Seth could hear the call.

"Quiet. Just the way I like it," Parker replied. "Your buddy Joe checks in on me now and again."

"How's school going?" Evan asked. After Parker left home, he started a program at the local community college and was working his way through, with help from Seth and Evan.

"Better. I think I'm getting the hang of it," Parker told him. "I've made some friends, and my job at the coffee shop is good. And yes, I'm wearing all the protective charms, and I keep the sigils fresh on my apartment."

Seth knew that being back in touch with Parker made Evan happy. Evan's family hadn't approved of him being gay, and his brothers had fallen out of touch until Parker sought him out just a few months ago.

"I actually did have a reason for calling besides news about my boring life," Parker said. "I've been digging into your next warlock's online footprint. Discreetly, I promise," he added, forestalling a warning from Evan.

"Fletcher Swain's whole 'wellness influencer' thing isn't just creepy —there have been a number of disappearances near his retreat, which happens to be in an area where it's mostly illegal to have cell phones, Wi-Fi, or most other radio signals," Parker told them.

"There is such a place? Why?" Seth asked, intrigued.

"It's called the National Radio Quiet Zone—NRQZ for short—and it's for scientific purposes and military intelligence gathering," Parker replied. "It straddles the West Virginia, Virginia state lines. There's a big observatory there, too. In some places, people who live near the zone can't even have microwaves."

"That's pretty hardcore," Seth said.

"The observatory has a good reason—radio astronomy—but it made me think that a crazy warlock mentor might not have the best intentions for luring people to his mountain retreat," Parker said.

"Please tell me you're not drawing attention to yourself," Evan begged. "You know you're still a target until we get all the witch disciples."

"I'm being very careful," Parker told him. "But the whole 'mountain mystic' gig fits right in with Swain's history as a shady preacher in his past 'lives.'"

The witch disciples gained immortality from their sacrifices. That required them to reinvent their identities periodically to avoid people noticing that they didn't age. They tended to stay in the same general area as the family of descendants they had chosen for their victims.

"Did you find anything about the disappearances? The warlock isn't the only reason people go missing," Evan said, and Seth could see how proud he was of his smart little brother. He felt a pang of loss for what Jesse could have become and figured that the grief would never go away.

"The NQRZ has been there for a while—since 1958—and they picked the location because that area is fairly remote," Parker said. "Not very populated and off the beaten track. I've been looking into the missing person reports going back as far as I can for the general area, especially the small towns nearby."

Parker seemed to relish sharing his findings. "Every year several people go missing and are never accounted for. They might not all be due to Swain, but you said he can draw power from blood magic in between his main sacrifices, so I think it's possible he's responsible for some of them. And a few have indirect ties to his retreat—people who left the program and later vanished, or who had other connections to his business. Nothing the police ever bothered with, as far as I can tell."

"Good work," Evan said. "Anything else?"

"I'm not sure," Parker said. "I found a link between Swain's charity and some fundraising groups that have gotten in trouble for dicey dealings."

"What kind of trouble?" Seth asked.

"Improper paperwork, tax issues, not following the rules," Parker replied. "I just found that piece, so I'm still looking into it, but it made me wonder if he had a hand in the other groups instead of just being associated."

"Be careful," Evan cautioned, and Seth knew his partner was walking the line between appreciating Parker's contributions and protecting his little brother from a very real threat. "Don't do anything that would attract attention to yourself."

"I won't." Parker sounded patiently put-upon. "I promise."

"Keep us posted. We'll be in Pittsburgh for a little bit before we head for West Virginia."

"Got it. I'll let you know as soon as I've got something to report." Parker paused. "You two watch your backs, okay? Don't get hurt."

Seth shifted his weight to ease the ache in his shoulders. Evan moved to take pressure off his bruised hip. "We will," Evan promised. "Talk to you soon."

The call ended. Seth and Evan exchanged a look.

"Thoughts?" Evan asked.

"He's good," Seth said. "Let's hope that he knows enough to fly under the radar. But if his hunches pay off, some of our friends might be able to dig into other sources to find even more information. Swain and the warlocks have had a century to learn how to cover their tracks. There's a reason no one's untangled this whole mess before now."

Seth and Evan had been searching archives for photos of Fletcher Swain under his various aliases without much luck. The best image was from 1900, the year Swain gained immortality. It showed a tall, thin man with light hair and sharp features. Later pictures tended to be blurry or a hat obscured the face, something Seth knew couldn't be completely accidental.

"Lucky us." Evan winced as he put pressure on sore muscles.

"Actually, yes."

Evan raised an eyebrow with a skeptical expression.

"I mean, first off it's how we met."

"I'll give you that," Evan admitted.

"And we've built a network of friends with special skills so we're not doing this alone," Seth pointed out. "That makes a big difference. And the payoff is that when we're done, no one else loses someone they loved to the coven's fucked up rituals."

They dozed on the couch before the movie was over and shuffled stiffly to the bedroom.

"I have one good hand," Evan offered with a smirk. "Wanna fool around?"

Seth groaned. "Yes, I want to. Not sure whether the rest of me is onboard, but I'm always in the mood for you."

"Slow and easy." Evan rolled onto his unbruised side and reached for the waistband of Seth's sweats. Seth's cock clearly was unaffected by the ache in his shoulders and woke quickly.

"Two hands are better than one," Seth murmured as he got the lube from the nightstand, slicked his palm, and reached into Evan's sleep pants to pull out his hard dick. Wrapping their fingers around both cocks together created delicious friction. Despite the dangers of the day, it didn't take long to push both of them over the edge.

"Best part of today." Seth cleaned them up with tissues from the box beside the bed. "Love you."

"Love you too." Evan sounded sleep-drunk and sated. "Rest up. I'm all for round two in the morning."

2

SETH

"I<small>F THERE'S EVER A ZOMBIE APOCALYPSE,</small> P<small>ITTSBURGH WOULD BE PRETTY</small> easy to defend," Evan mused as Seth drove into the city. "So many bridges and roads that cut through cliffs with high ground that have a perfect sniper view. Not to mention the rivers. Can zombies swim?"

"Do they have to? Couldn't they just sink to the bottom and walk across?"

Evan gave him a look. "Like in the pirate movie? I guess so. If there are slow and fast zombies, are there swimmers and sinkers?"

"I really hope I never have to find out." Seth maneuvered the Silverado through the narrow streets, grateful that they left the RV parked at a campground south of the city.

"Never hurts to be prepared. Didn't they shoot that George Romero zombie flick here?"

"Yeah, in Monroeville. Zombies in a mall. That's a classic," Seth said with reverence.

Evan shifted in his seat for a better view out the side window. "The city looks different without snow."

The last time they were in Pittsburgh, Seth and Evan hunted a witch disciple based there, right around Christmas. That was when they met Travis and Brent.

"Still cold," Seth grumbled. "And the hills of West Virginia are going to be cold too." He rolled his shoulders, trying to get comfortable. A good night's sleep and some ibuprofen eased the stiffness, but he knew it would take a couple more days before he and Evan could even think about going into a fight at full capacity. Given the stakes, he wasn't willing to take the risk of anything less.

"If we'd have headed to Savannah like we originally planned, it would be warmer," Evan pointed out.

"Yeah, but all the newest intel said the West Virginia warlock was likely to move his sacrifice up sooner," Seth replied. "So we'll be freezing our nuts off for a good cause."

"I solemnly swear to keep your nuts warm," Evan joked.

Seth maneuvered the truck into the parking lot behind St. Dismas, a halfway house in the Hill District. He spotted Brent's black pickup and Travis's old Crown Victoria, confirming he was in the right place.

Travis Dominick met them at the door. The ex-priest grinned in welcome and shook hands with a firm grip. Travis was in his early thirties, nearly as tall as Seth and Evan, with chin-length black hair and green eyes that contrasted with his pale coloring.

"Good to see both of you. Come in." He stood to the side to let Seth and Evan go first. "You need to see Matt? Looks like you're limping."

Seth nodded. "Yeah. We got tossed around by a ghost at a haunted hospital on the way here. Long story. We're both pretty sore."

"I'm sure he can get you on the schedule," Travis replied. "Follow me."

Travis once belonged to a secret Vatican group of demon hunters known as the Sinistram. He grew uncomfortable with the Sinistram's ethics and left both the group and the priesthood, despite considerable pressure to stay—and return. Now he hunted on his own terms and managed a small recovery program focused on second chances.

"Hey, Matt! I've got a couple of new ones for you," Travis called out when they reached the in-house clinic. St. Dismas provided food, shelter, basic medical care, counseling, and community for its residents. Matt Sanchez, a former army medic, handled the infirmary, while Travis and his site manager Jon took care of the rest.

"Seth and Evan! Good to see you again. What fucked you up?"

Matt greeted them with a big smile. He was also in his thirties, with a wiry build, thick black hair, and perpetual stubble.

"I'll be back when he's done with you." Travis excused himself. "Brent's already here, and there's coffee and donuts in the meeting room."

Seth explained the ghostly confrontation at the hospital, and Matt gave them both a thorough check, making sure no bones were broken or serious damage done.

"I know you're busy saving the world, but if you can spare a few days to heal, it would keep you from re-injuring the joints," he warned. "I can give you something for discomfort and inflammation. Ice will help. The best medicine is not doing any new damage until the old damage heals."

"We were planning to take a couple of days here before we head south," Seth said. "The witch disciple will be at the top of his game, so we need to be ready for him."

They thanked Matt and followed Travis to a no-frills conference room down the hall. St. Dismas had once been a hotel, and its origin showed in the layout. While the building wasn't fancy, fresh paint and good maintenance hid the flaws. Brightly colored accents and punchy but inexpensive art made the corridors warm and homey. Seth felt certain that Travis had a lot to do with St. Dismas's welcoming atmosphere.

Brent Lawson greeted them with handshakes instead of the usual backslaps, and Seth figured Travis warned him about their injuries.

Brent was around the same age as Travis, with short blond hair, blue eyes, and an athletic build. Despite having left the FBI years ago to become a monster-hunting private investigator, something about his manner still suggested "federal agent."

"Sometime you two need to come to Pittsburgh just to have fun," Brent said. "In nice weather, when you're not chasing ghoulies and ghosties. See a baseball game, eat pierogies, try some local beer. We've got it going on here."

Travis just shook his head and closed his eyes, resigned. "Ignore my partner's ill-advised attempt to be cool. But we have plenty to do and lots of good food."

"Seriously? The *priest* is giving cool lessons?" Brent bantered.

"*Ex*-priest. And yes. Because you need all the help you can get after so many years in those boxy suits with the high-and-tight hair." Travis's voice lacked heat. Seth always figured that for the two work partners, bickering was half the fun.

Seth and Evan helped themselves to coffee while Travis passed around the donuts. They chatted while they ate before getting down to business.

"Parker's chasing down a lead between Fletcher Swain's wellness empire and some shady online fundraising companies." Evan shared what his brother had discovered. "I'm thinking that his retreat in the no Wi-Fi zone is pretty suspicious, and likely to be where he does the rituals."

Travis took notes as they talked. "Yeah, I think that makes sense. I'll see if any of our contacts know more."

"I'm working with some folks to untangle the whole paranormal pharmaceutical cartel," Brent said, refreshing his coffee. "The warlock in Cleveland was deep into it. I don't think it's Fletcher's main focus, although he's probably involved."

The coven had found ways to prosper over the past century. Developing pharmaceuticals and recreational drugs adjusted to the metabolisms and body chemistry of vampires, werewolves, and other paranormal creatures was a thriving side business, one that Seth and Evan and their friends were making inroads into shuttering.

"Trafficking shifters and psychics doesn't seem to be Fletcher's deal," Travis chimed in. "But someone has to run the back office for their businesses, and there's plenty of money to be made in cybercrime. Everything we've found suggests Fletcher's the kingpin for those operations."

"We've gotten hints that there's a cybercrime hub operating out of Moundsville—which has the best internet speed in the state if you were wondering," Brent told them. "Wire fraud, money laundering, phishing, deepfake porn, and identity theft."

Evan let out a low whistle. "We're talking RICO territory here."

Brent gave a wolfish grin. "Yeah, For sure. Only someone needs to make the charges stick, and not have the judge get eaten before the trial."

"This isn't the usual boiler room kind of stuff," Travis added. "For identity theft, Fletcher's got shifters, wendigos, kitsune, and crocottas working for him. They can mimic voices and appearances to sound and look like anyone. Then you add in artificial intelligence, and it's a real nightmare."

"Holy shit." Seth and Evan exchanged a look. "That's some operation. You think Swain uses the wellness stuff to launder money?"

"It wouldn't surprise me," Brent replied. "And while Swain isn't in the thick of the drug ring, if that NRQZ area prohibits airplanes and drones, it makes surveillance a lot harder to rule out growing illegal and dangerous plants. After all this time, I don't think the witch disciples miss a trick."

"Parker said there'd been disappearances. I guess the local cops just didn't notice—or care?" Evan said.

"Oh, they notice, but they're paid not to care." Brent's voice had a sharp edge. "The FBSI has an office in Beckley, and I've still got a contact there from the old days. He's a good guy and one of the few who knows the score about things that go bump in the night. I'll give you his contact info and make sure he knows to look for you. He knows the territory, and he'd come in handy for backup. Just don't, er, actually kill anyone in front of him."

"We'll do our best," Seth deadpanned.

"Drake Carlson?" Evan asked.

Brent looked surprised, and Seth laughed. "Milo already suggested him—good you can vouch for him too."

"Let's say that we get rid of all the witch disciples," Evan spoke up. "Then what? They're at the top, but they're running a crime ring—there's a whole organization. Sure, we can stop the ritual murder of the posse descendants, but the drugs and fraud and trafficking—what's to keep someone else from stepping into their shoes?"

"Welcome to law enforcement," Brent muttered. "Cut off the head of the snake, ten more pop up. This is why it's so hard to bust the normal drug cartels and slimeballs. There's always a lieutenant to keep things going while the kingpin does time. Hell, some of these guys still run their empires from inside and have a limo waiting when they get out."

Travis kicked Brent under the table. "What my gloomy friend meant to say is that you do what you can and pass the ball when it's someone else's turn," he told them. "Stopping the coven is like taking out the bosses of a crime family. The underlings will be in chaos. Usually factions vie for power. They're vulnerable—sometimes weak enough to shut down operations."

"Think about how many lives will be saved just by stopping the witch disciples from taking their sacrifices—and their extra 'power boosts,'" Brent added. "Hundreds of people won't die, and families won't lose loved ones. That's a huge contribution. You don't have to stop all the bad guys everywhere."

Seth saw an expression of vindication cross Evan's face. *Is he worried that when we can finally walk away from all this, I won't want to give up the rush?*

Parts of the hunt were an adrenaline high, usually in the midst of a fight to the death. In Seth's opinion, the aftermath of shakes, nightmares, and PTSD wasn't worth it.

We risk our lives every time. It's been close more than once. Why would I take the chance that we'd lose our luck—and each other—for the thrill of the chase?

On the darkest nights, Seth considered walking away without eliminating the rest of the witch disciples. *Jesse didn't ask for vengeance.*

Then he remembered that although the warlocks had each "claimed" one of the posse's families, the ritual could be done with any descendant. That meant that he and Evan would never be safe until all of Gremory's acolytes were destroyed.

I need to listen more when Evan daydreams about what comes "after." And maybe we need to have a conversation about priorities. I don't want him to ever think that he's not at the top of the list.

Brent slid a folio across the table. "Here's everything I could find on Swain and his former aliases, as well as land ownership, deeds, and the rest. You've probably already got most of it, but sometimes it's that one odd extra detail that makes the difference."

"I don't visit the Duquesne Archive more often than necessary,"

Travis said with a look of distaste, "because they keep trying to drag me back into my old life. But I found a couple more banishment and exorcism rituals that don't require much magic or mediumship. Given how well both of you have done with rote spells, I think they'll work for you."

Both Seth and Evan had a small ability with magic, good for things like lighting candles and picking locks. Although they weren't flashy talents, those small spells had saved their asses more than once.

"I also got these from a friend." Travis held two small velvet bags.

When Seth turned out the contents—a silver charm in the shape of an ear—onto his palm, he felt a tingle of magic. Evan held an identical amulet.

"It's an *auris*," Travis said. "When you wear it, the charm protects you from liars, manipulators, and charismatic con men. I got thinking about how Swain's past roles have been clergy, tent revival preachers, televangelists, and now as a wellness mystic. They all hinge on him being able to sway people with his words and charisma. That is probably his flavor of magic, and he uses it as a weapon."

"Would it work against a used car salesman?" Evan turned the amulet in his fingers.

Travis laughed. "Actually, yes. Even more so if they used magic to 'nudge' you into a sale. All magical items have limitations, but these are powerful enough to give your common sense a chance to override his charisma, without any harmful effects to you."

"Thank you." Seth clasped the chain around Evan's neck and stood still for Evan to do the same for him.

They chatted for a while about some of Travis and Brent's recent hunts and traded news they had heard from other hunters.

"Can you stay for dinner?" Travis asked. "It's spaghetti tonight, and you don't want to miss our homemade sauce."

"I can vouch for the sauce," Brent said. "And don't worry about mouths to feed—he makes enough for an army."

"If you don't have anywhere better to be, it's game night. We always have a good time," Travis added.

Seth and Evan exchanged a look, and Seth nodded. "Sure. Except you have to let us help serve or clean up to earn our dinner."

"Deal," Travis replied with a broad smile.

The meal was as good as promised, homemade and filling. Seth and Evan took turns on the serving line and helped with clean-up. Game night took a page from speed dating, with classic board games set up at different tables and players switching after one session.

"I haven't played some of those games since I was a kid," Evan admitted when the evening finally came to an end. "My brothers were cutthroat. This was more fun."

They thanked Travis and Brent and headed back to the RV, more tired than usual thanks to the pills to treat their sore muscles. The campground had a hot tub that ran year-round, and by the time Seth and Evan soaked for a while they agreed that the damage from the fight at the old hospital was definitely getting better.

"Matt wanted us to take one more day slow," Evan remarked as they got ready for bed. "I have some ideas."

"Are any of them sexy?" Seth teased.

"Only if you're good."

"Babe, I'm always good," Seth couldn't resist the comeback.

Sleepy from the medication and the hot tub, they made out slow and easy, not in a hurry to take things further, and fell asleep tangled together.

"Matt said we should keep things low-key today," Evan reminded Seth over coffee the next morning. "He told me to switch off walking and sitting to keep from getting stiff, but that 'ambling' would help work out the tightness. So...let's go look at dinosaur skeletons."

They stopped for breakfast at a nearby diner, then headed back into Pittsburgh.

"The Carnegie Museum of Natural History," Evan announced when they reached the big stone Victorian building. "There's an art museum in the other wing and a huge conservatory next door. Plus a café. Just what the medic ordered."

They marveled at the massive dinosaur skeletons that had been reconstructed to loom over visitors.

"I'm glad we don't have to hunt those," Evan said. "Modern cryptids are a lot smaller."

True to Evan's word, the museum was perfect for trading off sitting and walking. Evan liked the gem exhibit, while Seth couldn't help geeking out over the Egyptian display and the many taxidermied animals. The café's sandwiches, coffee, and sugar cookies were better than Seth expected, and he enjoyed the rare chance to breathe and indulge in an unhurried recovery day.

"Did you go to museums as a kid?" Evan asked Seth as they wandered through the sculpture court in the adjacent art museum.

"On school trips and once in a while on vacation," Seth replied, unable to keep from gawking at the gigantic archways and statues.

"Mom and Dad liked museums," Evan said wistfully, "because they were educational. We usually got something at the gift shop if we were good. I've always wanted to go to some of the really big ones, like the Met in New York or the Field Museum in Chicago."

"Put it on the bucket list for when we're done." Seth gave Evan's hand a surreptitious squeeze. "We can go anywhere you want when this is all over."

We just have to make it out alive.

They meandered through the art exhibits, and Seth felt an unusual sense of peace settle over him as they quietly debated what they saw in the different paintings, sometimes with hilariously different interpretations. Their RV didn't have much room for knickknacks, but Evan couldn't resist an apron with Munsch's "The Scream" as a souvenir.

Phipps Conservatory didn't disappoint. Its huge glass greenhouses seemed like something out of a Victorian movie, filled with tropical palms, fragrant flowers, and hundreds of orchids. Seth stole a kiss behind a giant fern frond, surprised at how romantic the setting was.

"You know how to plan the perfect day off," he told Evan.

"We're not done yet," Evan assured him. "We have dinner reservations at this family-run Italian restaurant that got top ratings for food and date night, and then on the way back we could take the incline train up to the overlook. I've seen pictures of the view of the city at night with the three rivers—it's pretty amazing."

The pasta fra diavolo and chicken marsala were as good as the reviews promised, and the intimate setting seemed perfect to hold Evan's hand under the table. After polishing off homemade tiramisu, Seth felt relaxed for the first time in a long while.

"It's still early," Evan said when they got back in the pickup. "Let's go to the overlook."

The Monongahela Incline was a small red single train car that went up and down a steep set of tracks to the top of Mount Washington from the street below. At the summit, a large balcony looked out over downtown Pittsburgh. The city lights reflected from the swift dark waters of the rivers in a vista that made Seth catch his breath.

"Wow." He stood close behind Evan, braving the chill wind for the majestic view.

"I know, right? It's even better than the pictures," Evan replied, excitement clear in his voice. "Can you imagine what the Fourth of July must look like up here?"

They were alone on the overlook, so Seth placed his hands on Evan's hips and pulled him back against his chest. "We don't do this kind of thing often enough," he said. "I'm sorry. I promise to do better."

It's been nothing but blood and fighting and death since we ran off together in Richmond. I keep telling myself that "it's only until we finish the job," but that's no way to live. I'm so lucky to have him with me, and I love him so much. I swear I'll find a way to make this right.

"I know what we're doing is important, but I want happy memories along the way." Evan leaned his head back on Seth's shoulder. "They take the sting out of the bad days."

"You're the best thing that ever happened to me," Seth murmured. "Thank you."

"You saved my life, so you're stuck with me," Evan teased. "I'm right where I want to be."

A gust made Seth shiver, and he reluctantly led Evan back to the incline. They were alone in the car, and looked out over the skyline as they descended.

"Hard to believe that a hundred years ago, people called Pittsburgh 'hell with the lid off' because of the smoke from the steel mills," Evan said.

"Thank you for today." Seth sat close enough that they touched from hip to knee. "I didn't know how badly I needed this."

"Thanks for going along with it. And Matt was right—my hip feels a lot better. The arm is still sore, but not as much."

Seth nodded. "My back's still tender, and the bruises will take a while to fade, but definitely improved. Let's go back to the RV and give the night a very happy ending." Seth licked his lips for emphasis.

"I think that could be arranged." Evan bumped his knee. "I have a few ideas for that too."

Seth had stopped praying when his family died, but sometimes he found himself still asking the universe for a favor and hoping someone was listening. *Please let us cross the finish line together, one way or the other.*

3

EVAN

"CHURCH CAMP AS A TEENAGER WAS NEVER LIKE THIS." EVAN TREAD carefully over the uneven ground of the abandoned complex, shotgun racked and ready with salt rounds in his right hand and an iron knife in his left.

"I went skiing. Does that count?" Seth tossed back.

Evan snorted in response. "Not unless they did après ski altar calls."

The decaying retreat grounds made him jumpy, even though they hadn't seen any ghosts—so far. Ramshackle bunk houses loomed at the edge of the compound, just inside the treeline. A central gathering area had once held a large firepit and seating circle, of which little remained. The main building, which probably housed the cafeteria, multi-use spaces, and offices, looked to be in somewhat better shape than the other structures, although Evan wouldn't trust the roof not to come down on him.

Camp Morning Glory brought up memories Evan preferred to leave buried. His family hadn't been fanatically religious until his father realized they were "cursed" to lose the oldest male of each generation. With no way to know about the witch disciples' vendetta, Evan's father had decided that some unknown sin had doomed them and threw the family into religious devotion to atone. Which made Evan's coming out even worse than it probably would have been.

"This must have been a fairly nice place long ago. There are amphitheater seats cut into the hillside over there." Seth pointed. "And what's left of a stage. It looked like there might have been a pool on the other side of the main lodge."

Evan nodded, recalling what he had found online. The camp turned up many times over the years in Buckhannon history, usually connected to tent revivals and traveling evangelists.

Overhead, branches rattled in the wind. Evan looked around, staring into the shadows beneath the trees, almost expecting eyes to be looking back at him. For now, at least, the forest seemed empty.

"I guess before television and computers, there wasn't much to do in these parts. A big revival with lots of singing and emotional speeches was probably the most exciting thing to happen for months," Evan replied, trying to shake his mood.

He had been to the modern-day equivalent of Camp Morning Glory and knew that all of the good stuff—music, games, food, and camaraderie—came with a heaping helping of guilt and manipulation. The kind of preachers who drew crowds were gifted speakers who knew how to stir emotions and sway an audience, and in Evan's experience used those talents cynically to line their pockets and enhance their power. Swain would have been even worse given his magic.

"Swain had a good con set up," Seth agreed. "He'd probably do the speaking himself for a while, then take a decade off to reinvent and have his underlings sub for him before returning as a hot new attraction once people had forgotten his face."

Inside one of the decrepit bunkhouses, something crashed, making them jump.

They exchanged a look. "If a tree falls in the forest..." Evan said.

"Yeah. This place has been decaying for years. No reason for it to stop on our account," Seth replied, but Evan heard a note of uncertainty in his voice.

Seth took a folded paper from his pack and spread it out, orienting it by his compass. Evan looked over his shoulder. They had found a map of the camp as it had been not long before it closed, and while changes and additions had been made over the decades of operation, Evan hoped it would provide enough of a guide for their purposes.

The girls' cabins lined the left side of the compound, with the boys' on the right. Larger cabins for families dotted the back. A stone archway straddled the entrance, leading to a fountain with water pouring from an ancient-looking vase. The arch survived, but the fountain lay in cracked ruins.

Off to one side was the main building, which also held the staff offices. Behind it was a pool, which Evan shuddered to think of investigating. Behind the cabins on the boys' side was a basketball court and tetherball, with a tennis court and a playground beyond the girls' lodging. An outdoor gathering place with amphitheater-style seating had been cut into the hillside beyond the family lodging.

An expansive open space ran up the middle on the other side of the fountain. From the map, Evan noted that it once held a firepit and a tall brick belltower. Tucked into a space in the back corner was a contemplation labyrinth made from cut stone set into the ground. Walking trails had once rambled through the woods, leading to a small shrine, and the old map showed a pond, dock, and picnic shelter just a short walk from the main facilities.

"I know they built onto the camp over the years, but this must have been a nice place back in the day," Seth mused. "Probably as fancy a 'vacation' as a lot of the folks who came here ever had."

"Swain never had a church of his own," Evan recalled. "He was a traveling guest speaker, and he put on revival events in the towns all around here. If his magic involves charisma, maybe he was able to draw energy off the crowds he gathered in addition to the power boost from his sacrifices."

They had learned that while the sacrifice of the posse descendants fueled the continued link to Rhyfel Gremory's trapped spirit, other ritual murders provided a lesser—but still potent—source of energy.

For a long while, they believed that killing the descendants of the sheriff and his deputies was a form of tribute from the witch disciples to their master. Only recently had they discovered that the truth was even more sinister. Gremory's soul remained trapped between life and death. When the disciples sacrificed a descendant, the energy opened a portal to Gremory's prison, drawing from his magic and perpetuating his suffering.

The reality was ghoulish. Evan felt torn between satisfaction that Gremory had indeed been punished for all the pain he inflicted on so many others and queasy at the thought of any creature being tortured for eternity.

He'd had enough of that sort of thinking before he left the church.

"You're right about Swain," Evan continued their earlier conversation. "All the money he collected was tax-free, and the authorities would have been afraid to touch him even if they heard about disappearances. They wouldn't want to go against a man of the cloth." He didn't bother to hide the bitterness in his tone.

Seth seemed to pick up on his mood. "Hey." He jostled Evan's arm. "Leave the past in the past. You're out. Parker's out. We're together. Don't let what happened back then tangle up your thinking about what's going on with Swain now."

Evan gave a curt nod. "I know. I'm trying. But it's hard. The past feels closer here."

"From what I could find, he's moved up in the world with his retreat center in the NRQZ," Evan said as they tromped around the old campgrounds. "Took over an old resort hotel. It's not far away, but definitely classier. He's good at funneling money through non-profits to keep his fingerprints off the cashflow."

"Guess he got tired of roughing it." Seth kicked a branch out of his way. "You see anywhere around here that might be where he stashes his anchor?"

Each witch disciple had a relic that helped them store and boost their magic, as well as an amulet that enabled them to focus and control that power. While they tended to keep the amulet on them, the warlocks often stored the anchor in a safe but accessible place between rituals.

"If it's here, I'd start with the bell tower and move on to the buildings. But before we search those, we need to have better gear. Hard hats, safety lines, the works," Evan noted. "And that doesn't account for any magical traps he might have set."

"Hmm. Both the camp and the retreat center are still within the

NRQZ here. The new lodge might be more convenient, but I doubt anyone comes here much, so I could make a case either way for where he might stash the anchor." Seth turned, looking at the grounds around them. "Lots of people full of belief and hope came through here for decades. It's the sort of thing that the ground remembers."

"Isn't it a little too quiet here?" Evan realized that the normal bird-songs and underbrush rustlings had gone silent.

"That's never a good sign." Seth scanned the treeline.

The darkened cabin windows, most without their panes, reminded Evan of skulls with empty sockets. Evan wasn't a medium, but he'd learned long ago to trust his intuition. The longer they stayed at the campground, the more oppressive the feel of the place became. It didn't escape his notice that the place was named after something beautiful but deadly.

Was Swain toying with everyone, even back then? Hiding in plain sight?

He was always a con man, taking advantage of easy marks. How many other ways did he abuse their trust? He stole their money, took advantage of their faith and goodwill, and carried out ritual sacrifices. Did he take other liberties? Plenty of men in those positions did.

Evan had heard rumors back in Oklahoma. Those who spoke up about such things found themselves as unwelcome as Evan had been when he told his own truth.

"I don't think we're wanted here." Evan watched the shadows, expecting ghosts to make themselves seen at any moment.

"Yeah, I'm getting that feeling," Seth agreed.

While the camp was still in use, two drownings had occurred in the pool. Through the years, a handful of people had gone missing in the general area, written off as runaways. Evan suspected that the real story was much darker and that local officials didn't want to look too closely at Swain's "ministry."

There have got to be ghosts here. Are they hiding from us? Could they make themselves visible if they wanted to?

"Let's see if anyone wants to talk." Seth pulled supplies from his bag. He spread a tarp on the ground that was marked with runes and sigils along the edges. In the middle of the tarp, Seth made a circle from a rope soaked in salt, holy water, and colloidal silver, marking a space large enough for both he and Evan to sit.

As Evan kept watch, Seth lit candles at the four quarters of the circle and withdrew a Ouija board from his bag.

"Not fancy, but it works." Seth shrugged and got into a comfortable position. He took a deep breath before staring straight ahead into the shadows.

"Ghosts of Camp Morning Glory—we wish you no harm," Seth said as Evan constantly scanned for any sign that the revenants were listening.

"We apologize for disturbing you, but we need information about a man who might have done you harm—Fletcher Swain. He's gone by other names, and he used to run this camp. We want to hold him to account. If you can help us, please make yourself seen."

Evan found that he was holding his breath. The odd stillness seemed to deepen, and his skin itched with the sensation of being watched.

The temperature dropped, turning cold enough for Evan to see his breath. He saw staticky flickering in the air around them, as if spirits tried to make themselves visible but lacked the power to do so.

"Thank you for coming," Seth continued, and Evan guessed his partner sensed the spirits' presence. "If you can hear me, give me a sign using the talking board."

Seth let his fingers rest lightly on the planchette. As Evan watched, the raised triangle quivered, then moved slowly to the word "yes" on the board.

"What are your names?" Seth waited to see if the triangle would move again.

Very slowly, the marker spelled out names: "Amy," then "Cathy," followed by "Kenny."

While last names would have been helpful, Seth had more questions, and they didn't know how much energy the spirits could maintain.

"Good," Seth encouraged and drew the planchette back to the center of the board. "Was your death an accident?"

The triangle moved fast this time, circling the word "no" so vigorously that it felt like a silent shout.

"Was Fletcher Swain involved in your death?" This time, the triangle remained still. Seth began to list the other names Swain had gone by during his unnaturally long life. Once again, the planchette darted to "yes."

"Holy shit," Evan murmured. He didn't know how many ghosts answered Seth's summons or whether more than one chose to respond via the Ouija board. Whatever they learned this way wouldn't be admissible as evidence, and they were likely to have difficulty corroborating the ghosts' testimony.

"Did Swain kill you?"

"Yes," the planchette indicated.

A chill skittered down Evan's spine. He didn't think the ghosts meant them harm, but then again, some had been at the camp for a long time, with decades to reckon with the injustice done to them. That made him wonder whether the camp had become so haunted that Swain had abandoned it.

"Did he kill you here?" Seth asked.

It seemed as if ghostly hands tugged at the planchette, arguing over the answer as the triangle veered wildly between "yes" and "no."

"Are you buried here?"

Once again, the spirits vied for control, giving both answers.

Maybe some of them had families that claimed the bodies. Or they died here, and he moved the corpses elsewhere.

"Does Swain come back here?" Seth probed. Evan knew he was looking for a lead on where the relic might be stored.

A cold wind stirred dead leaves and whistled through the warped boards on the ruined cabins. Evan tried to move in a slow circle to keep them from getting blindsided. Frost formed on the broken windows, and the clang of rusted windchimes sent an eerie note through the stillness.

The planchette juddered as if it were alive, finally spelling out "not now."

"When did he stop?"

Evan suspected that the spirits had grown restless. Whether they were running out of energy to interact or were troubled by the memory of their killer, Evan had a gut feeling that their time was running out.

The planchette moved sharply enough that it jerked out of Seth's hand, rapidly moving from one letter to another. "R-U-N."

"Shit," Seth muttered as an icy wind guttered the candles. The gray static of the ghosts abruptly vanished, and the shadows from beneath the trees seemed to grow darker.

"Is that a ghost?" Evan asked as his heart pounded.

"I don't think so. Not sure what it is, but nothing good."

The rusted chimes clattered and banged like a claxon. A gust howled through the old buildings, banging broken boards, fluttering loose shingles, and driving away the salt line.

Both men wore a collection of protective amulets made of silver, onyx, agate, and specially woven cords imbued with magic. They were a first defense, but not body armor. Evan helped Seth stuff his equipment into the bag and they ran back the way they came.

Evan chanced a look over his shoulder. Shadows closed in over the common area where they had been just moments before, far too quickly to be a trick of the light. He didn't know what the darkness was, but primal instinct screamed in his hindbrain that to be caught by it would be very, very bad.

He stumbled over a tree root and pitched forward. Seth grabbed his wrist in a vise grip and pulled him along, never breaking stride.

Plunging through the archway sent a frisson of energy through Evan, tingling along every nerve. The forest felt different, without the wind or ominous air pressure. Seth turned on his heel to face the campgrounds.

"Spirit of darkness, depart! You have no welcome here. Be gone, and trouble this place no more," Seth commanded, drawing on his ability to banish ghosts as well as call them.

His minor magic wasn't full mediumship like what Travis could do. This time, Evan feared Seth's skill wouldn't be a match for the evil spirit.

On this side of the arch, Evan heard the distant song of birds and saw shafts of sunlight through the branches overhead.

Beyond the arch, a billowing shadow obscured the cabins and bell tower. A sharp crack like a breaking branch cut through the stillness. Seth continued his chant, with one hand tightly gripping the blessed silver charms around his neck.

The longer Seth chanted, the wilder the wind grew, like a counterpoint to his words. Seth's voice rose above it all.

"Go, and do not return!" Seth finished, shouting with authority and triumph.

The shadows screamed and then tore apart, losing color and substance until they drifted away like smoke.

Evan ran to Seth when he looked ready to collapse. "Are you okay? That was pretty impressive."

Seth nodded and gratefully accepted the bottle of water that Evan dug from the bag. "Yeah. I just might not have much of a voice left. Damn, I wasn't expecting that."

"Was that a demon?"

Seth frowned and shook his head. "I don't think so. We'll call Travis tonight and run it by him, but binding and controlling a demon takes a lot of energy, especially to guard a place no one comes to. That kind of ongoing drain would be hard to maintain."

"Then what?" Evan felt breathless as the adrenaline surged through him.

"There are dark entities aside from demons and ghosts," Seth replied. "And it's interesting—whatever it was didn't seem to really trigger until I reached out to the ghosts. So my bet is that if hikers stumbled upon this place and passed through, nothing would happen. But if someone uses magic, however small—"

"You know we're going to have to get back in there to look for the anchor," Evan said, although that was the absolute last thing he wanted to do. "And if the boogeyman reacted to a Ouija board, you can bet he's going to be pissed about us rooting around looking for a magic relic."

"Let's see what Travis says and go from there." Seth picked up his bag and slung it over his shoulder but kept his shotgun in hand.

"When we deal with Swain, maybe we can find someone to cleanse the spirit of the land and help the ghosts move on," Seth suggested. "Let's get out of here."

Despite having the heater on in the truck, it took Evan a while before he felt warm. The chill of the old campground seemed to go down to his bones.

They ate lunch at a local Mexican place, delighted to discover excellent homemade tamales, tostadas, and empanadas. Evan couldn't resist the bottomless chips and salsa, which he washed down with a cold Coke.

"Let's get a look at Cameron." Seth named the warlock's next target. "He works at a casino. Maybe we can get a sense of how well he'll deal with us trying to save his life."

In Evan's case, Seth's first attempts hadn't gone over well. Past experience had made Evan wary, and despite his attraction to Seth, he had resisted believing in the supernatural and refused to accept that he was in danger from a dark coven with a century-old grudge. His inability to trust nearly got them both killed until he finally realized Seth was telling the truth.

Evan felt his cheeks color at the memory. Seth nudged his knee under the table as if he guessed the direction of Evan's thoughts. "You had good reasons to be skeptical. Any sane person would be. Let it go."

He nodded and tried to push the feelings away. Since then, Evan had done his best to embrace Seth's quest to stop the coven's killing spree. They had saved lives, both in the present and for future generations. That didn't make explaining the situation to a newcomer any easier.

They paid the bill and walked back to the truck. Evan pulled up the casino on his phone and frowned at the photo. "Not exactly the Bellagio."

"Maybe it's a bad photo." Seth pulled out of the parking lot. They didn't have far to drive and found themselves in front of Lacey's, a squat blue and white cement block building sporting neon beer signs in its front window.

"Looks more like a strip joint," Seth said. "I'm guessing they've got video machines and a bookie, maybe a backroom with poker."

"And here I was, hoping for Cirque," Evan snarked with an exaggerated sigh.

"Add it to the bucket list."

Evan figured Lacey's passed for an "entertainment complex" in the area. A bar lined one wall with multiple screens showing live sporting events, horseracing, and several online multi-player betting games. Four poker tables took up the center, leaving only a few places for patrons to eat. Video gaming machines flashed and blinked along the far side of the room. A small stage off to the right sported a pole, but the amps and drum set suggested that sometimes bands played.

"I guess they've cornered the nightlife around here," Seth murmured.

"It's a long drive to go anywhere else," Evan agreed. "They're probably making the most of that."

Evan had worked his share of bars. He knew where to look to judge how well a place was run. He felt vaguely surprised to find that Lacey's looked clean and well-maintained, if somewhat hard-used. The health certificate on the wall vouched for the food. The state allowed smoking indoors at casinos, but Evan figured the place must have a decent air handler since it didn't reek.

Cameron Davis didn't spend time on social media, but his friends did. That had yielded some photos and a vague idea of his interests and habits. Evan spotted Cameron behind the bar as soon as they entered. Cameron was in his early twenties, with a face that was pleasing, if not quite handsome, and reddish brown hair cut in a style just a few years past trendy.

Watching Cameron at work, Evan could see that he was an experienced barkeeper. He flowed from one patron's order to another with no wasted movement, using the tricks of the trade that shaved precious seconds off during busy times. Evan figured the other man had either gone to bartending school or been doing it long enough to learn the hard way.

Despite being early afternoon, Lacey's wasn't empty. Two older men nursed beers at the bar, deep in conversation. Four of the video machines were taken by retirees who looked like they'd probably been on the same stools since the joint opened.

Evan made a slow tour of the machines, ending up at the bar. "Got any hard cider?" he asked Cameron, who appeared to be the only bartender on duty.

"Yeah, but only one brand," Cameron replied without looking up.

"Good enough." Evan laid cash on the bar. "Is there a menu?"

Cameron snorted in amusement. "Lunch specials are two types of cold sandwiches with chips and a pickle. After five, we've got burgers, fries, wings, and pizza."

"Okay." Evan took a drink from the cider bottle. Seth meandered up to the bar beside him, flagged down Cameron, and ordered a beer.

"Anything I need to know before I pick a machine and try my luck?" Evan watched Cameron as he worked, gauging how the other man handled distractions. So far, he seemed like a pro.

"If someone gets up, make sure they're really gone before you snake their machine. Mrs. McHenry cracked a guy's skull once with a purse full of quarters when he tried to take her lucky spot," Cameron answered. "We have dancers Thursday through Saturday, live music most Sunday nights. Last call is at 10:30. We close at eleven."

"Thanks," Evan replied. "Sounds like you've given that speech before."

"Maybe a time or two." Cameron wiped his hands on the bar towel hanging from his apron. "What brings you and your buddy in? I thought I knew everyone in town."

Evan fiddled with the cider bottle, drawing his finger through the condensation. "We're in the area for a while and heard the food was good."

If Cameron had doubts about Evan's story, he kept them to himself. "Lacey's is a classy joint for these parts. You could do worse. A word to the wise—just be careful where you get your barbecue. Pick the wrong place, and you could have a heap of regrets."

"I'll take that advice to heart," Evan said. "You from here?"

Cameron shrugged. "Buckhannon? Yeah. Been here at Lacey's for a few years. Like I said, it's a nice place. The owner's an above-board kind of guy; the regulars don't throw up in the bathroom, and we haven't had a brawl since the last time WVU lost to Penn State."

Evan finished his cider and ordered another before heading for the machines. Seth stayed at the bar, and Evan figured his boyfriend would find a way to ask a few questions. Evan picked a machine where he could watch the bar in the mirrored backdrop, keeping an eye on both Seth and Cameron.

"That's it! Keep it coming!" the older lady at the machine beside him cheered. Lights and bells signaled a win. Evan smiled, enjoying her enthusiasm. Gambling had never held any fascination for him, although he had gotten to be a much better poker player thanks to Seth.

He started a game, but his attention was split watching his surroundings. They had agreed to stake out Lacey's to get a feel for Cameron and the bar's patrons. Unlike the old camp, Evan didn't get a bad feeling about Lacey's. He'd been to some seedy places, tended bar in a few during his leanest times, but Lacey's lacked their bone-deep sense of despair.

A few hours later, more men trickled in. Most sat at the bar, and it was clear from their cheers or groans that they were betting on the games. Seth played the machines for a while, then got a poker game going. Between practice, skill, and a penchant for counting cards, Evan knew Seth could probably hustle the whole bar, but he trusted his partner not to get them thrown out.

Evan's thoughts drifted to Seth's "bucket list" comments. *That's new. He didn't use to talk about "after." When he started the hunt, I'm not sure Seth expected to survive destroying the coven. Then we got together, and now there's a future. I want to make it over the finish line with him. We've earned a happily-ever-after.*

When he couldn't make himself play another game, Evan gave up his seat and walked back to the bar, moving close enough to the guys watching sports and cheering for their teams. He suspected that betting added to their investment in the outcome.

I've got enough stress hunting dark witches. I don't need anxiety over a stupid game.

Seth joined him a few minutes later, patting his pocket to let Evan know he had walked away from the table a winner. He settled his tab and left a generous tip.

"You sold us on this place," he said to Cameron. "We're in town for a few days. We'll definitely be back."

Once they were back in the truck and Seth had pulled out of the lot, Evan shifted in his seat to look at him. "Well? What did you make of him?"

"Seemed like a decent enough guy in that he wasn't an asshole," Seth replied. "I didn't pick up even a tingle of energy, so I doubt he has any magic of his own."

"How hard do you think he'll be to convince?"

"Depends on whether he's noticed the pattern and thinks the family deaths aren't quite right. Guess we'll find out once we break the news."

"Where are we going?" Evan asked. "The campground is back the other way."

"I'd like to hit the local library. We found a lot online, but little towns don't have a budget to digitize everything, and the volunteers aren't likely to go back through decades of old records. Now that we have a couple of names, maybe we can find out more."

"That's not much to go on," Evan warned. "And over a century of records."

"It'll help if we start with the missing persons reports. Buckhannon isn't a big place."

"The people who disappeared might not have been from here," Evan pointed out. "Back in his preacher days, Swain moved around a lot."

"Gotta start somewhere. I don't think the names of the ghosts match what Brent found. So it's worth a shot. We might find connections."

Evan stayed back while Seth sweet-talked the librarian into giving them access to the microfiche room and the public records. Seth shot him a wink as they followed her to the lower level and waited while she unlocked a door.

"Prop the door if you need to go to the restroom, or it will lock behind you," she warned. "No eating or drinking; don't make any marks on the pages. There's a copier, but it only works part of the time, and coins get stuck. You're better off taking photos on your phone."

The first two hours found no matches, which didn't surprise Evan.

Seth focused on the area right around Buckhannon while Evan looked further afield. One set of records caught his eye.

"I didn't realize it was so close," he muttered, intrigued.

"What was?" Seth looked up from his stack of records, blinking like he was chasing away the need for a nap.

"The Trans-Allegheny Lunatic Asylum. It's become quite a tourist attraction."

"Sounds like a lovely place," Seth remarked, sarcasm thick in his voice. "Haunted as fuck, I bet."

"Definitely." Evan's voice trailed off as his thoughts ran ahead of him. "I wonder…"

Seth watched him for a moment as if expecting him to finish his sentence. When he didn't, Seth returned to paging through his documents until Evan gave a muted shout of triumph.

"Find something?" Seth took a deep breath and stretched back in his chair.

"I found an Amy Johnson and a Kevin Adams who were patients at the asylum back in the day. They were just teenagers, locked up on what looks like bullshit 'diagnoses.' Their records say 'died while trying to escape'—like that's not ominous."

"The hospital's been closed for a long time," Seth noted.

"Amy died in 1925, and Kevin died in 1932. And get this—one of the hospital chaplains during that period was Pastor Eli Fletcher."

"One of Swain's aliases."

"Uh-huh. Hell, that would have been like shooting fish in a barrel." Evan was angry at Swain's abuse of trust to prey on patients who had no recourse.

"I've found a couple of women named Cathy—or some version of Catherine," Seth said. "The one I think is most likely is a teenager who disappeared in 1943 who got off a bus in Buckhannon and was never seen again."

Evan sat back in his chair. "And those are just the ghosts who could communicate through the Ouija board. I bet there were others who either couldn't make it work for them or didn't want to try."

"Yeah. Pretty sure of it."

"But why?" Evan asked. "They aren't from the deputies' families, so they aren't right for the main sacrifices. Do you think he's been doing 'power boost' murders all along?"

"Why wouldn't he?" Seth countered. "No one was looking for a preacher to be a murderer, and people would be hesitant to say anything, even if they saw suspicious evidence. A lot of people sent to those hospitals had been given up on by their families. No one was looking out for them, and no one cared when they disappeared."

As depressing as Seth's assessment was, Evan knew he was correct. This wasn't the first time the dark coven had taken advantage of people who slipped through the cracks.

Seth's phone rang, and Evan recognized the ringtone.

"Hey, Travis. Miss us?" Seth asked with a smirk as he put the call on speaker.

"Like athlete's foot," Travis joked. "You get to Buckhannon in one piece?"

"Mostly," Evan replied. "With an adventure or two along the way." He glanced around, but the lower archive floor looked deserted except for the two of them. He gave a brief accounting of their trip to the old campground.

"You were lucky," Travis said. "Even with proper preparation, a vengeful spirit like that can do serious damage."

"Do you know any mediums in the area who might be able to help? We think there are more ghosts who couldn't use the Ouija board, and we need to go back to look for Swain's anchor," Seth said.

"I don't know anyone near there, but you're only a little over two hours away. Brent and I are happy to come down and help if you want the company."

Seth and Evan exchanged a relieved glance. Evan figured they had both been trying to figure out whether to ask.

"That would be great," Seth replied. "There's a lot here to unpack between the cyber issues and the skeevy retreat. We could use the help."

"Have you met the target?" Travis asked.

"Yeah. Seems like a decent guy—Joe Average. No indication he has any clue about what's going on," Evan said. "We're keeping an eye on him in case Swain decides to move up his timeline because we're in the area."

"Do you know whether Swain tracked you?"

"We're going on the assumption that he has because the warlocks seemed to keep tabs on each other, so we figured he'd be watching for us," Seth said.

"Probably not wrong. If Swain is aware of you, then coming to town might move up his schedule on the next victim," Travis pointed out.

"That's happened before," Evan admitted. "But what's the option? If we delay, he might still move the timetable or kill other 'power boosts' in the meantime."

"You don't have any good options," Travis agreed. "So we need to move fast."

"We're going to shadow Cameron and figure out the best time to explain," Seth said. "We don't know if Swain is already watching Cameron, but my bet is that he's got him in his sights."

"Just be careful—remember you and Evan aren't out of the woods yet," Travis warned.

The call ended, and Evan gave Seth a quizzical look. "You okay with reinforcements?"

"Sure. We've nearly had our asses handed to us enough times. I'm not going to turn down help—especially from guys like them."

"Good." Evan was secretly relieved. He had thought about suggesting they work together when they visited in Pittsburgh but worried Seth might be uncomfortable asking for help.

After another hour, they had compiled a list of people who had gone missing from the area around the camp, the asylum, and the forest near the retreat. For a place that wasn't thickly populated, it seemed to have more than its share of disappearances.

I bet the cops write it off as teenagers leaving town on their own. Either they don't want to bother, or they know who's behind it and don't want to cross him.

They left the library and drove around the area to get the lay of the land. The entrance drive to the Mountain Laurel Lodge was marked with an unassuming sign, indicating that the retreat itself was several miles from the main road.

"They weren't kidding about 'remote,'" Evan observed. They were well outside of Buckhannon and had driven a while without even passing a gas station.

"Pretty countryside," Seth noted. "I did a search on the observatory at the heart of the Quiet Zone. They're doing some interesting research, reading signals from deep space. I can understand why they want to keep the human noise to a minimum."

"I usually like to avoid human noise whenever possible," Evan replied. "And it's not that people aren't allowed to live in the area—there are just restrictions they have to follow if they do. For off-the-grid types, I don't imagine that's a problem."

Despite the ominous overtones of the hunt for the witch disciple, Evan had to admit that the mountains and valleys were gorgeous. The trees were losing their leaves, past their prime for color but not yet bare. He tried to imagine what the slopes and gorges looked like in the lush green of summer.

"It would be nice to come back this way when we're not tracking a psychotic killer," Evan said. "Not necessarily *here*, but somewhere in the mountains. Get a cabin with a hot tub, sit on the porch with a good book when it rains, maybe get a look at Sasquatch."

"If we see him, do we have to shoot him? Because I'm not cool with that," Seth joked. "Live and let live when we're off the clock unless he's a were-squatch, and then all bets are off."

Once night fell, they stopped at a Waffle House for dinner. The steak and hash browns weren't fancy, but they were filling, and with bottomless coffee refills. Stopping at the chain was a guilty pleasure when they traveled through the South.

"You boys here for the retreat?" Lisa, their server, asked. Evan guessed she was about his mom's age, with short blond hair and a red lipstick smile.

"You mean at the lodge?" Seth played along.

"Yeah, the old resort that got fixed up and turned fancy," she replied.

Evan shook his head. "No. We're just passing through. What kind of retreat?"

Lisa refilled their coffee while she talked. "Some sort of New Age-y meditation yoga thing, I think. Don't know more than that. They don't really advertise to the locals. I guess people come in from all over. I hope they spiffed the place up, because I remember going to a wedding before the old lodge closed and it wasn't much to write home about."

"Is it a church thing?" Seth knew that answer, but Evan figured his partner wanted to find out what the locals thought.

"Not that I've heard tell. Local folks worried when it opened that it might be some kind of cult, but it seems to be a hipster thing, sit around and watch the clouds," Lisa replied.

Evan suspected there was a lot more involved, but Lisa—and probably others in the area—had come up with an explanation that appeased them, and they didn't seem inclined to look into the matter more deeply.

"Do you know who runs it? They must be someone pretty famous to have a place like that." Evan finished his coffee, and Lisa poured a refill.

"Nobody I've heard of," she replied, unconcerned. "I imagine there're records at the courthouse about who bought it, but the retreat people keep to themselves, and we don't bother them."

Evan thought he heard a warning in her tone for them to steer clear. "Thanks for the info. You never know what you'll come across when you travel."

"That's the truth. You boys ever seen the World's Largest Ball of Twine? Who comes up with these things?" She walked away, shaking her head.

"I think we've just had the most Waffle House conversation ever," Seth said, watching her go.

Evan laughed. "I was thinking the same thing." He finished the rest of his coffee, and they paid the bill.

Once they were back in the truck, Evan continued. "Did you notice how it seems like people are going out of their way to not pay attention to the resort? If a fancy place that might pay well opened up in a small town, you'd think people would be lining up for jobs, or at least to get a peek at goings-on."

"Yeah. My bet is that even though they don't know the whole truth about Swain, they know enough to stay out of his way," Seth replied. "Makes me real curious to scope it out—once we make sure Cameron's safe."

They headed back to Lacey's Bar and parked just beyond the lot where they could keep an eye on the door without being obvious.

"This could be a waste of time," Evan pointed out as they sat in the darkened truck. "We don't know when Swain intends to strike."

Seth shook his head. "No, Travis is right. We set things in motion by coming here. Even if Swain hated his coven brothers by now, he'd know that six of them have been destroyed. The other witch disciples know who we are. So Swain has to weigh moving up his timetable for the sacrifice or risk Cameron getting spooked and running away."

Lacey's lot stayed full until almost closing time. Evan figured the gambling had a lot to do with the popularity, along with the lack of competition. One by one, the cars finally began to leave and the light-up sign went dark. Seth and Evan waited until Cameron and the kitchen staff came out the back door beneath the glow of the security light.

Cameron and the others walked to their cars, and Evan watched their quarry get into a Honda CRV.

"There he goes," Evan said as the CRV pulled out of the deserted lot.

They waited until the small SUV passed before Seth turned on his lights and eased out of the spot, making a U-turn to follow. He hung back, trying not to be obvious, hoping that a black truck blended in, given the rural area.

Cameron drove at a steady speed, giving no indication that he knew he was being followed. He pulled to the curb near a small house on a quiet street and turned off the car. The streetlight overhead had burned out, leaving the area dark.

"Something's off," Evan said.

"I think you're right."

Cameron got out of the SUV and locked it, heading to the house a short distance away. Movement in the shadows attracted Seth's attention as two men clad in black came at Cameron from the front and the back, boxing him in.

"Go!" Seth and Evan sprang from the truck, running toward where Cameron fought to fend off his attackers.

Cameron struggled, but he was losing. Seth went after the man who pinned Cameron from behind while Evan closed on the other man trying to grab the bartender's legs.

Evan tackled the assailant, taking them both to the ground, hard. He didn't see a gun, but he wasn't taking any chances. They had left their weapons locked in the truck, which he regretted.

"Who sent you?" Evan punctuated his question by slamming the man a little harder against the sidewalk.

"Fuck you," the man growled, doing his best to throw Evan off. Out of the corner of his eye, Evan saw that Seth had managed to pry Cameron loose from the other guy's grip.

"Run!" Seth yelled.

Cameron bolted for the house as Seth and the attacker traded punches.

The man Evan pinned rolled them hard to the side, throwing their combined weight onto Evan's sore hip. His grip faltered for just an instant, but it was enough for the assailant to tear himself free.

Seth's opponent got in a lucky punch that staggered him for a moment. Together, the two men sprinted into the night.

"Shit. You okay?" Evan climbed to his feet.

Seth rubbed his jaw. "Yeah. You?"

Evan froze as he saw a man he didn't recognize heading their way with a gun drawn.

"Don't move!" the man ordered. Evan saw Cameron hovering worriedly on the porch. "Now you're going to tell me who the hell you are—and who the fuck those guys were—and why you showed up here."

"Someone wants to kill Cameron—just like he's killed other men in Cameron's family." Seth cut to the chase. "We're here to stop that from happening."

"That's crazy." The man holding the gun looked to be in his early twenties like Cameron, with long, dark hair. He was shorter than Evan and Seth, but solidly built and carried himself like he'd been military.

"It's the truth," Evan replied. "But it's a long story. Put the gun away, and we'll tell you more."

The gunman hesitated. Evan really didn't want to explain the situation to the local cops and feared that was what the other man intended.

"Tyler—stand down. They saved me. I'd like to know why," Cameron called from the porch. Evan looked around, hoping that they hadn't attracted the attention of any neighbors who might be tempted to dial 911.

"You've got one chance to explain yourselves." Tyler lowered his gun. "Go sit on the porch. If I don't like what I hear, I'm turning you in."

Tyler shoved the gun into the back of his waistband and walked behind Seth and Evan toward the house. He gestured for them to sit on the swing while he and Cameron stood.

"You were at the bar." Cameron sounded surprised. "What's going on?"

"We're trying to save your life," Seth replied. "The same person who killed your father—and your grandfather's older brother—is coming after you. We're here to stop that."

"What a pile of bullshit," Tyler snapped.

Cameron held up a hand. "Hold on." He turned back to Seth and Evan. "Tell me what you know."

"You can't be serious," Tyler protested.

Cameron turned to him, his expression a mix of fondness and frustration. "Ty—I want to hear them out."

Tyler swore under his breath and turned away, walking a few paces but staying close enough to come to Cameron's defense if needed.

Cameron turned back to Seth and Evan. "All right, I'm listening. Make it good."

4

SETH

"Start over." Cameron sat on a chair facing the swing. Tyler stood behind him, making it clear Seth and Evan were on limited time. "Who were those guys? Why do you think they jumped me?"

Seth took a deep breath and jumped in feet first. "A hundred years ago, one of your ancestors was a sheriff's deputy outside Brazil, Indiana. Their posse hanged a dark warlock—a real, honest-to-god wicked witch. His coven swore vengeance on the posse and their descendants. They each chose a deputy's family. Twelve witches, twelve deputies."

Cameron looked thoughtful, but Tyler's expression made it clear he wasn't buying the story. Seth knew he had to convince both men or their rescue effort would fail.

"The witch disciples created a ritual around killing the deputies' descendants, and that gave them a big power boost," Seth continued. "For a long time, they were careful. One sacrifice each year, rotating among the witch disciples and the descendants. Lately, they've started to grab more power, so no one's safe."

"Come on, Cam. Are you buying this shit?" Tyler protested.

"It's true," Evan spoke up. "I'm a descendant. I didn't believe Seth's story at first, either. But they blew up my apartment. I got kidnapped and dragged inside an old tunnel. I was nearly gutted, and then I saw a big hole in reality open. I figured Seth knew what he was talking about. Seth is a descendant too."

"They killed my brother," Seth said. "And I made him a promise that I'd stop the rituals forever. We've dealt with six of the warlocks. Six more to go."

"By 'dealt with,' you mean—" Tyler said, unconvinced.

Seth looked up and met his eyes. "*Handled.*" He read Tyler as being ex-military and brought that piece of his own background full-force into his manner, just so they understood each other.

"You're psychopaths," Tyler snapped. "Cameron, we don't have to listen—"

Cameron gave him a look that wordlessly cut him off. "He's making sense, Ty. There's stuff you don't know—that I was hoping I never had to tell you."

"What the fuck?" Tyler slapped the back of Cameron's chair in anger and frustration and turned away, swearing under his breath before pivoting. "Like what?" he shot back at Cameron with a look of doubt and betrayal.

Cameron cleared his throat. "I didn't tell you because I didn't want it to be true," he said quietly, cheeks reddening with shame. "It got drilled into me not to tell people. But what he's saying matches the stories in my family, only they say we're cursed and that an evil spirit kills the oldest male of each generation."

Tyler's expression shifted from doubt to fear in a heartbeat. "You're the oldest."

Cameron nodded. "Yeah. So was my dad. He was a long-haul trucker. He died twelve years ago in an accident no one could explain. I remember him saying that his uncle—the oldest—also had strange circumstances around his death."

"Did your family ever try to stop the...curse? Call an exorcist or something?" Tyler asked. Seth figured it was a good sign that the other man had stopped mocking and was asking real questions.

"This is a small town," Cameron said. "People here still believe D&D gets people demon possessed. I think my mom went to the next town to talk with a priest, but I got the feeling it didn't go well."

"It usually doesn't," Seth commiserated.

"Mom went to church—a lot. Methodists aren't very prepared to deal with curses. There were crosses all over the house, and she gave all us kids St. Michael's medallions—slayer of Lucifer and all that." Cameron dug under his shirt and withdrew a silver disk on a chain.

"That's actually useful," Evan pointed out. "Silver works against a lot of ghosts and supernatural creatures. It's probably providing a low level of protection—better than nothing—but it's not enough to hold off the warlock."

Evan drew out the cluster of amulets that hung from a strap around his neck. "Amulets work, but certain runes protect for specific circumstances."

"How do you know all this stuff?" Cameron asked.

Seth didn't usually dive right into his own painful story, but winning Cameron's trust was going to take complete honesty.

"After my brother was killed, my parents died in a car wreck, and the house burned in a suspicious fire. I decided I was going to stop the warlocks from destroying anyone else's family—or die trying." Seth was surprised that he no longer felt a surge of devastating grief revisiting the details.

That'll come tonight, with the nightmares.

"I was lucky enough to find mentors who knew about this kind of thing, and that's why I didn't get myself killed right off the bat," Seth continued. "They taught me enough to get started. I taught Evan. We've learned on the job since then."

"Do you know who the warlock is?" Tyler asked. "Are you certain? You can't just go around putting a stake through people's hearts."

"That's vampires," Evan replied. "Not warlocks."

Tyler gave him a side-eye. "Vampires?"

"Not important right now," Seth said.

Tyler glared at him. "I'd say it's very important. Are they real?"

Seth let out a long breath, shut his eyes, and nodded. "Ghosts, vampires, and many of the creatures in urban legends are all real. But whatever you've seen in the movies is mostly wrong."

Seth had given what he thought of as "the talk" to many people who found their lives disrupted by supernatural dangers. Some were more receptive than others, usually if they couldn't deny their own experience. He didn't fault the skeptics, who were lucky enough to be able to walk away and ignore an uncomfortable truth.

"My grandmother on my dad's side was very superstitious," Cameron ventured. "I'm not sure it did much good since Dad still died, but she was always making odd marks near the doors and windows and spreading salt on the sills and front step."

"Right idea...but got the details wrong," Seth said. "Salt repels ghosts, and protective symbols can keep certain...entities...away. But most of them won't hold off a witch—especially not one as powerful as this one."

"You still haven't told us who," Tyler pressed.

Seth was hoping to avoid that part until they had won Cameron's trust. The last thing they needed was a misguided report to the local police.

"He's effectively immortal, so over the past hundred years he's gone by many names. Most recently, Fletcher Swain." Seth admitted.

"He's immortal?" Tyler challenged. "Then how do you 'handle' him?"

"We disrupt the ritual when he's opening a portal to the trapped soul of his dead master and push him through," Evan replied in a matter-of-fact tone.

"Do you have any idea how crazy that sounds?" Tyler argued.

"Yep," Evan said. "And I almost got both Seth and me killed because I didn't believe until I nearly got bled dry and tied onto an altar like something out of the late show. 'Crazy' doesn't mean 'not real.'"

"If he's a witch, why send hired muscle to grab me? Can't he just hocus-pocus me to his secret lair?" Cameron sounded flippant, but Seth sensed a serious question under the bravado.

"Magic is hard work," Seth replied. "It takes a lot of energy to do even small things. Big spells can drain a practitioner without proper preparation. That's one of the things TV and movies get wrong—their witches just go zap-happy and never run out of mojo. It's like how guns on television never run out of bullets."

Tyler snorted in amusement at that, something Seth knew was a constant annoyance to people who knew their way around weapons.

"A smart witch avoids wasting energy," Seth continued. "So they hire human muscle. Relatively cheap, disposable, and replaceable. He'll either pay for their silence or put a geas on them to compel obedience and discretion. That's a lot less magic than poofing you off the street."

"Go back to this wicked warlock being Fletcher Swain. You mean the wellness mentor guy who bought that haunted old lodge on the mountain?" Cameron asked.

Seth almost missed the flicker of emotions that crossed Tyler's face. Discomfort, recognition—and fear. *There's a story here. Maybe Tyler isn't quite the non-believer he pretends to be.*

"That's the name he goes by now," Evan replied. "The problem with immortality is that people notice if you never age. So he's cycled through several names over the years and leaves the area in between sacrifices until people forget about him."

"Swain's a big deal." Cameron shot a look at Tyler, who evaded his gaze.

Definitely a story behind that reaction.

"He's supposed to have a huge following online, but no one ever sees him," Cameron continued. "I guess if you pay for his retreats, you get to meet him, but he doesn't allow cameras. I heard someone say that Swain says photographs 'drain his energy.'"

Seth snorted. "Well, that's one way to keep from being recognized."

Evan looked to Tyler, who had gone quiet. "You seemed uncomfortable when the retreat center came up. Have you heard something?"

Tyler and Cameron traded a look. Cameron gave a slight nod, conveying support.

"I worked at Mountain Laurel Lodge the first summer after I got out of the Army while I figured out what I wanted to do," Tyler said. "I thought I was tough. I'd seen combat. I figured the worst that could happen was catching some guests doing drugs or fucking each other." He shook his head. "Turned out that wasn't true."

Seth and Evan waited, letting him tell the story at his own speed. Seth appreciated that Tyler was willing to risk sharing something he felt conflicted about. That Tyler didn't sound like he told the story easily added credibility.

"I'd grown up around here. There have been a lot of stories about the Mountain Laurel Lodge. People say crazy things. One rumor said that the man who built it back in the 1950s had been a hitman for the Mob and retired with a big payout. Other people said there used to be a village up there that got wiped out by a monster, and the resort was built on their graves. And then there were the stories about celebrities who overdosed or jumped off balconies or tragic love triangles that ended badly. I really didn't pay any much attention," Tyler said ruefully.

"Once I got there, I learned fast that the staff took the ghost stories seriously. They told me rooms to watch out for, hallways to avoid at certain times, places I should never go. I thought it was a hazing. You know—like sending someone snipe hunting," Tyler went on, coming around to sit next to Cameron. "So I ignored them. I mean, I'd just come from a deployment where we worried about air strikes and suicide bombers and IEDs. I wasn't going to get scared off by ghost stories."

His voice grew quieter, and he looked down at his clasped hands on the table in front of him. Cameron laid a hand on his forearm in silent support. Tyler's wan smile flickered in response.

"At first, I didn't see anything weird. I didn't go looking for the spots they said to stay away from. I was too busy to mess around like that, and nothing took me to those places. I kinda forgot about the stories."

Tyler's jaw tightened. "Then I had to cover some night shifts because we were short-handed. One of the guys just left his keys and badge on the check-in counter and never came back."

"Did anyone ever see him again, or did he really just run away?" Evan asked.

"I don't remember. I was just glad to get some extra hours," Tyler said. "The duties were a little different, and they took me into some of the areas people said to avoid. I didn't think much about the weird cold spots because it was an old building. But there weren't a lot of people in the service corridors in the middle of the night, and it started to spook me that I kept hearing footsteps when no one was there."

He met Seth's stare. "I thought I saw a woman in a long dress going up the employee-only stairs. I called out to her, thinking that maybe a guest got lost, but she didn't respond. I was watching her, and she just vanished," Tyler went on. "There wasn't a door for her to go through. One second, she was there, and the next, she was gone."

He took a few breaths. Cameron rubbed the back of Tyler's neck and murmured something Seth couldn't hear.

"I thought the others were pranking me since it was my first night shift. But I couldn't figure out how. I didn't hear anyone running away or snickering. And there was something about the way the room felt when I saw that lady that really creeped me out," Tyler confessed. "So I kept working. I heard footsteps a few more times, but I convinced myself that it was just someone else running an errand. Then I got turned around—I was still pretty new—and I ended up in the wing that hadn't been remodeled yet."

"I'm still not sure how I got there. Some of the lights didn't work, the wallpaper was peeling, and the carpet stank. I figured it had to connect with the new part, so I kept walking. Then I saw a man ahead of me in the shadows. Or at least, it was the silhouette of a man. I called out to him, asking how to get back to the main section," Tyler added, growing quieter.

"When he turned around, he didn't have a face. I was scared, but I still thought I was being pranked, so I made some stupid insulting comment about leaving me alone. And then..." Tyler licked his lips and paused. Cameron squeezed his shoulder.

"Then it *stretched* toward me. It didn't walk or float—it just expanded. And I got the same gut feeling that I used to get in the Army when things were going to get really bad. I knew that if the shadow touched me, I'd be in big trouble. So I turned tail and ran. I flew out of there as fast as I could, back the way I came." Tyler was breathing fast, and Seth heard shame in his voice.

"It was behind me—until it wasn't. I didn't care. I kept running until I found my way back to the main area. My boss saw me—I must have looked like a wild man—and he didn't say a word, like he knew. He fucking *knew*."

Tyler drew in some slow breaths. His hands clasped into fists on the table. "I worked the rest of the summer, but I never took night shift again." He shook his head. "I tried so hard to convince myself it wasn't real, but I know it was."

"There was that other time, too," Cameron prompted. He reached out and took Tyler's hand, lacing their fingers together.

Tyler looked at Cameron, who nodded that it was okay.

"Now you're really going to think I'm nuts," Tyler said self-consciously.

"We won't," Evan swore. "Promise."

"Yeah—you haven't heard me yet," Tyler said. "One time they sent me into the sauna to bring fresh towels. It was at an odd time, so I thought the steam room was empty. A guy comes out stark naked, and I stepped behind a curtain so I didn't embarrass him. And then his skin melted away."

"What do you mean, 'melted'?" Seth leaned forward. Tyler's initial resistance now seemed more due to trauma than skepticism.

"It went gooey, like a hot candle, and then just sort of…rearranged itself…until he looked like a completely different person," Tyler said. "I was so scared I nearly shit myself. I stayed real quiet, and he didn't notice me. He just went and got dressed, and I waited until he was gone before I threw up and went out for a smoke. I would have taken a couple of shots if I could have."

"Shapeshifter," Evan said. "They're not usually that sloppy about changing where someone might see. He must have thought he was safe—or that someone would cover up if anyone did see."

"I didn't tell my boss," Tyler said. "Ghosts are one thing, but melting people? I thought he'd either fire me for making up stories to get out of my duties or call the preacher, and I'd be getting prayed over at a camp meeting. Cam's the only person I ever told—until now."

Seth looked up. "Have either of you ever heard of Camp Morning Glory?"

Cameron frowned. "The old abandoned tent meeting place? I've heard stories about what it was like back in the day, but it's been shut down for a long time. Why?"

"Remember when we said that Swain had to change his name every so often to keep people from realizing that he was immortal?" Seth asked. "He was the preacher who started that camp and ran it for a long time. When he stepped away to change identities, he was still involved behind the scenes. What kind of stories do the locals tell about it?"

An ambulance siren shrilled, interrupting them until it passed by, lights flashing.

"Let's go inside," Cameron said, and to Seth's surprise, Tyler didn't object. "I doubt the neighbors are listening, but let's not give them more of an earful than we already have."

The 1930s house had an arts-and-crafts feel with dark wood trim, stained glass transoms, and an elaborate mantle over the fireplace in the living room. Modern furniture and accent pieces made the room feel eclectic instead of stiff.

Seth hadn't known Cameron had a partner until the brawl in the street. That fact made the job of protecting him easier in some ways—and more difficult in others. A target with a lover was more likely to take precautions instead of resisting protection. At the same time, it meant needing to convince—and protect—two people instead of one. While Tyler seemed to be listening, Seth figured he might be the more difficult to persuade, although his clear devotion to Cameron gave him a reason to pay attention.

"Your house is lovely," Evan said. "It has a lot of personality."

"You mean it's 'old,'" Cameron said with a laugh. "Thank you. Buckhannon doesn't have a booming real estate market and not much new construction. This was my grandmother's, and she left it to me. I always loved the woodwork."

He gestured to the living room, and they followed him. "You asked about the camp," Cameron said.

Seth and Evan settled onto the couch, leaving wingchairs for the others.

"Can I get you a cup of coffee?" Cameron asked. "I keep a fresh pot all the time. I practically run on the stuff." Seth and Evan took him up on the offer and waited with Tyler while Cameron went to the kitchen. He returned a few minutes later with three mugs. Apparently Tyler wasn't as much of a fan.

"A lot of folks in these parts have nostalgia for it because it offered the closest thing to a vacation many working people in these parts were likely to get. So I understand that. But there were things that went on that aren't popular to acknowledge. Mom and Grandma used to tell stories about it." Cameron settled into his chair with his drink.

"Like what?" Evan paused to sip his coffee.

"People went to the camp because of the music and potluck meals and to hear a speaker who got them all fired up," Cameron said. "Gave them a high like going to a big concert. There wasn't much else to do. So if folks got some Jesus with their excitement, they didn't mind because it wasn't like they were going to do anything differently come Monday."

Seth noted Cameron's cynicism and couldn't fault him. He'd seen that sort of thing himself, and Evan had lived it.

"Of course, the preachers never took on the coal barons who didn't pay fair wages and ran the company towns with unsafe mines or the Pinkertons who busted up the strikes. Those folks were too dangerous to preach about. So they had to find their 'sin' somewhere else," Cameron said.

"Way back in the day, praying out demons was a big draw," he added. "They'd drag in some poor woman who probably had mental health issues or a medical condition that caused strange behaviors and did this whole elaborate ritual to cast out the demons they said were making her sick," Cameron said with distaste. "People would drive from far and wide to see that."

"Of course, it was all huckster stuff," Tyler put in. "But that didn't stop them from passing the hat afterward."

"There were rumors that sometimes a kid's parents would drag him for a private session with the preacher to drive out 'impure' thoughts," Cameron went on, and his lip curled at the phrase. "Which probably meant he got caught jacking off, or his folks thought he might be gay.

"My grandma told me that there were whispers about the deacons getting handsy with the girls. Seemed like every year, one or two teenagers 'ran off' during tent revival season. Some people said they joined up, like with the circus. No one seemed to look for them real hard."

"Religion is a big deal in these parts," Tyler spoke up. "It's all the hope most folks have. This is a coal town in a coal region. The mining companies rule like kings—always have. A lot of people don't have much to show for a life of hard, dangerous work. The church has always done a better job of promising that things will be better in the afterlife than making them better in the here and now."

"Mines aren't the only thing under the surface here," Cameron added. "Lots of stuff stays buried in the dark. Plenty of secrets and a barrel full of lies. So the idea that Fletcher Swain might be a dark witch who practices human sacrifice is kinda on brand."

"And yet you both stayed." Seth sipped his drink and waited for Cameron to go on.

"For now," Cameron said. "I did the Culinary Arts program at the community college because it was all I could afford. Then I lucked into the job at Lacey's—the only place around here with decent tips. I was waiting for Tyler to come back from the Army, and then we figured we'd leave town, maybe go to Pittsburgh. Somewhere with possibilities."

"I just got out a couple of months ago," Tyler said. "With my experience, getting a job in law enforcement or security won't be hard—but not here."

"Why not?" Evan asked, although Seth suspected they both knew the answer.

Tyler snorted. "Old boys' network. Everyone knows that the local bigwigs have the cops in their pockets. Those folks can do no wrong. Other people don't seem to catch a break."

"So you were planning to leave town fairly soon?" Evan asked, with a look to Seth that spoke volumes.

"Tyler's already looking for a job in Pittsburgh. Getting a stint as a bartender shouldn't be too hard for me," Cameron replied. "Thought I'd rent this house out for more income."

"Have you said anything to anyone about leaving?" Seth asked, picking up on Evan's unspoken train of thought.

"A couple of people. Didn't want to say anything out loud until we were set," Cameron answered. "My boss won't have any trouble finding a replacement with two weeks' notice. Ty's been subbing as a security guard at the mall while he puts in applications."

"If Swain found out you were planning to leave, he would have moved up his timeline," Seth warned. "He wouldn't want you to slip away. He probably knows we're here—and that we're looking for him. We're going to have to move pretty quickly on this—and until it's settled, you're in danger," he told Cameron.

"What am I supposed to do? I can't just quit work."

"So you'll have a bodyguard. One of us," Seth indicated Evan, Tyler, and himself, "will be with you all the time. It's not fool-proof, but it does make snatching you more complicated."

"We've got some friends with special experience lending a hand," Evan added. "They can add additional protection."

"For how long?" Cameron looked nervous. Tyler's expression suggested that he took the threat seriously.

"A few days," Seth replied. "Was tonight the first time someone tried to attack you?"

Cameron's hesitation drew a sharp look from Tyler. "It was, wasn't it?" Tyler asked.

"I thought once or twice I was being followed or watched," Cameron admitted. "I didn't say anything because I wasn't sure, and nothing happened, so I figured it was just my imagination."

"You could have been taken, and I wouldn't have had any idea what happened to you," Tyler snapped. "I didn't even know there was a reason for you to be in danger."

Seth could identify with Tyler's protective anger. He and Evan had plenty of close calls. He took it in stride for himself, but the thought of Evan at risk made him seethe.

Cameron held up his hands, palms out, in a gesture of appease-ment. "That was wrong of me. I realize that now. Please, don't be angry. I've told you everything. We've just got to figure out how to live through this, and then we'll get out of town and never look back."

Tyler nodded, tight-lipped, indicating that the argument was over —for now.

"Tyler, you're on guard duty tonight," Seth said. "We'll put protec-tions on the house. They won't stop a full-on magical assault or a nuclear bomb, but I don't think Swain is ready to be that visible, at least not yet."

"What kind of protections?" Cameron looked interested.

"You have any salt?" Evan asked. "It repels ghosts and some other types of magic. I'll put it down at the windows and doors. Make sure you don't break the line."

"I'll mark sigils on the doors and windows that will also neutralize magic that isn't full blast. No matter what you see or hear, don't go outside until morning," Seth told them. "Step outside, and the protections won't work."

"What about tomorrow morning? I need to get to Lacey's."

"One of us will pick you up," Evan said. "We'll tag team until we figure this out and stop Swain."

They finished the protections while Cameron and Tyler watched. Before they left, Seth reached into his pocket and withdrew two medallions.

"These will help when you're not in the house," Seth explained. "They deflect minor magic. It won't save you from a direct, full power strike or a curse, but it should keep you from being affected by spells intended to confuse you or to make you let down your guard. Please wear them all the time."

They left with assurances that Cameron and Tyler would follow instructions, although both men looked a bit stunned over having their whole view of reality shifted.

"Do you think they believed us at the end?" Evan glanced back at the house through the side mirror as they pulled away.

"I hope so. It seemed like it," Seth said. "We dropped a lot on them. Considering everything, they didn't run screaming into the night, so I'll take that as a win."

Evan chuckled. "They're doing better than I did."

Seth shrugged. "Everyone's different. It seems like both Cameron and Tyler had some prior experience with 'weirdness,' which made it easier for them to believe. And eventually, you came around."

Evan rolled his eyes. "Yeah, after we both nearly died. I'm so sorry."

Seth reached out and took his hand. "Quit beating yourself up over it. That's all in the past. We're alive and together—and narrowing the list of witch disciples. Keep coming up with those bucket list ideas. We'll get there."

They checked the campsite warily, making sure none of their wardings on the RV had been disturbed and assuring themselves that no one lurked in the shadows. Once they got inside and energized the protections, Evan closed the distance with Seth and kissed him, hard and hungry.

"I trust you. You know that, right?" Evan breathed between kisses.

Seth's hands came up to frame his face, and he pulled back far enough to see Evan's eyes. "Of course I do. What's all this about?"

Evan kissed him again, deeper and with intent. "Making up for lost time—and old doubts."

"There's nothing to forgive." Seth guided him toward the bedroom. "But if you want reassurance, I've got ideas."

"Want to be close to you." Evan tugged at Seth's T-shirt and pulled at his belt. "Want to feel you everywhere."

They left a trail of clothing between the door and the bed, tumbling naked onto the comforter together. Evan's hands moved constantly, running along Seth's sides, cupping his ass, sliding over his chest as if he was reassuring himself of Seth's presence.

"I'm here. Not going anywhere without you," Seth murmured. "Slow down and enjoy the ride."

Seth landed on top, and Evan spread his legs to allow Seth to lie between them as they touched and kissed. Seth sensed that tonight was as much about reassurance as it was horniness, so he willed his boner to be patient, which was only partially successful.

He shifted, letting their cocks line up together as his hips began slow friction that sent heat up his spine. Evan moaned. "Just let me," Seth coaxed. "Tell me what you want."

"Anything. Everything. Just want to feel you."

Seth slipped his hand between them, smearing their cocks with pre-come and wrapping his fingers around them. "I'm right here. Stop thinking and just feel." Seth peppered Evan's shoulders, neck, cheeks, and forehead with kisses before returning to plunder his mouth. Their tongues slipped together, echoing the rhythm of their hips.

"Seth—" Evan's warm release covered Seth's hand, and his seed followed as he climaxed seconds later. They lay together, sticky, sated, and panting as Seth let the afterglow wash over him.

"That was...."

"Yeah," Seth agreed. "Feel better?"

"Uh-huh." Evan sounded sleepy and blissed out. "Tomorrow morning, I want you to fuck me."

"Sounds like a perfect way to start the day," Seth agreed. "But if we don't clean up, we'll be stuck to the sheet, which is not perfect in any way."

He gently disentangled himself from Evan's sprawled body and padded to the bathroom to wash up, returning with a warm cloth.

"I've got you." Seth washed away the spunk and sweat. Sometimes the aftercare seemed more intimate than the act itself. He took his time, making it a sensual ritual. The smell of sandalwood soap mingled with other low and earthy scents. "Good?" He tossed the cloth in the direction of the bathroom.

"Real good," Evan replied, nearly boneless as he let Seth maneuver him until they were both under the covers. Seth drew Evan against him, letting Evan rest his head against his shoulder and wrapping his arms around him.

They would inevitably get too warm and move apart, but Seth sensed Evan's need for contact and was happy to oblige.

"Go to sleep." Seth kissed the top of Evan's head. They were the same height, but somehow Evan seemed to be able to make himself seem smaller when he wanted.

Evan was one of the bravest people Seth had ever met. Despite their rocky start, once he had committed to Seth and the hunt for the warlocks, Evan had thrown himself in with his whole heart. He knew his lover's jitters weren't second thoughts or a change of heart. Some nights the weight of what they were doing seemed heavier, the ending too far away, the costs frighteningly close. He'd taken refuge in Evan's arms many of those times himself.

Every time they came up against one of the warlocks, there was the very real possibility they might not walk away. Seth tried not to dwell on that, and for the most part, he was successful. Maybe it was his military training or just his stubborn nature. That didn't always work, but it served more often than not.

"Shh. Just rest. I'm here. Let me take care of you."

Evan kissed Seth on the chest. "I love you."

"Love you too," Seth replied. "Now go to sleep so we can wake up and boink like bunnies."

5

EVAN

EVAN MADE GOOD ON HIS PROMISE TO START THE DAY OFF WITH HOT, SLOW sex, a last chance to indulge before the hunt for the warlock became all-consuming.

He was the first through the shower, and by the time Seth joined him, Evan sat at the table with a half-eaten bagel and his second cup of coffee, staring at his laptop.

"Something new?" Seth bent down to steal a kiss as he headed to get a mug.

"Parker's been researching Swain's wellness cult and sent a report. Unfortunately, all the gadgets he could build that might be helpful will also violate the Quiet Zone and show up like a sore thumb to the authorities."

Parker had a gift for re-engineering electronics into pieces useful for the special requirements of what Seth and Evan needed, gleefully invoking memories of the *Inspector Gadget* cartoons he had loved as a kid.

"Too bad. He's really good at that stuff," Seth noted. "I'm glad he's gone back to school."

"Me too. He just needed to get away from the family to shine."

Seth toasted a bagel and brought his breakfast to sit beside Evan.

"Show me what you've got."

Evan clicked open a video. "These are from the resort. Swain bought the old Mountain Laurel Lodge and remodeled it, calling it 'Summit' and holding his Renou-Vous wellness programs there. Parker's been combing through their website and anything else he can find online. He's not sure whether the stuff he found was recruiting new customers as much as creating social proof that Swain is a big deal."

"Interesting. Let's have a look."

The first video featured sweeping panoramic views of the mountains around the lodge, then photos that revealed an updated midcentury resort. Calm music and a woman with a soothing voice talked about learning to leave the cares of modern living behind, find inner peace, let go of doubt, and discover the path the cosmos intended.

Seth and Evan sat back when the clip ended, still staring at the screen. "Pretty words and nice pictures, but that's just a warmed-over secular version of 'go to church, and your life will be perfect,'" Evan said.

They watched a few more videos which followed the same theme. Seth frowned. "I'd love to get Travis's input since I think there's a trace of magic in the voice-over. If someone watched a lot of them, I think there's a low-key hypnotic suggestion going on that isn't entirely mundane."

"I didn't get the feeling that Swain wanted a following from the masses."

Seth shook his head. "That's not what I meant. But if local people or authority figures watched these, they might come away with the warm fuzzies enhanced by a touch of magic. Makes them less likely to look hard at any discrepancies or tolerate people who do."

"I also notice that Swain isn't in the video. He's quoted, and they mention him being the teacher-in-residence, but there aren't any pictures. Mighty convenient," Evan noted.

"Parker also sent a bunch of other stuff—I'm guessing he signed up for information on a phony account. There's a brochure about the resort itself with a map and floorplan—we should ask Tyler where the creepy places were."

"They might have finished renovating it by now," Seth pointed out.

"Maybe not, unless they're at full capacity. I have a feeling Swain would prefer a smaller number of easily influenced guests than a mob who might be harder to control."

"You're probably right," Seth agreed.

"And look at the comments on the videos." Evan scrolled down to show him. "They're not just good reviews. They're like the testimonials people used to give in church about how their lives had gotten turned around because of the saving power of grace. They're true believers—or well-paid PR flacks. Maybe some of both."

"Swain's got charisma—and magic. And he's been swaying crowds for a century. He knows just what buttons to push to have them eating out of his hand," Seth muttered.

"I asked Parker to see if he could find ties between Swain and the local power brokers—mayor, police chief, bank president, business and tourism organizations. I'm sure he's got them in his pocket, but it would be nice to know for certain," Evan replied.

"I don't think we can count on any local help, except that guy Milo and Brent told us about, Drake," Seth said. "I was hoping that once Brent and Travis got here, we could meet him and cook up a plan."

"Oh yeah? What do you have in mind?"

Seth rolled his shoulders and let his head fall from one side to the other, working out tight muscles. "Mainly, divide and conquer. You and I need to go back to the camp and find Swain's anchor if it's there. Cameron needs a bodyguard. We also need to check out the resort and that cyber hub in Moundsville that Brent mentioned. Even with help, that's a lot of territory to cover."

"Maybe Brent and his FBSI friend can have a look at the Hub," Evan suggested. "That's in the agent's purview, and if it does include creatures who can impersonate people, Brent knows how to deal with it."

"Yeah, that's what I was thinking. You and I can take Travis with us to the camp to see what else the ghosts can tell us. Tyler and I can have a look around the resort. And when it's your turn to keep an eye on Cameron, maybe you can teach him the finer points of research and take him back to the library."

"Sounds like a plan—although it never works out as smoothly in real life. And speaking of which—we promised to pick up Cameron," Evan pointed out.

"Let me grab coffee to go." Seth stood and carried his dishes to the sink. "I also thought I'd try my hand at hacking into Swain's cyber hub."

"Won't he have magic protecting it?" Evan filled his travel mug.

"Maybe. There is such a thing as Ensorcelled Encryption. But magic and electronics don't usually mix well," Seth pointed out. "It's one thing to ward the server room from the outside. But trying to spell-protect the actual circuits and programs? That would be a lot harder."

"You said the videos might have a magical touch." Evan added sweetener to his black coffee before tightening the lid.

"In the videos, a spell could have ramped up the charisma and appeal of the speaker, putting the person in a receptive state. Sort of like being hypnotized on a light level," Seth explained. "I don't think they could use magic to make people do things just because they watched the video. But I don't know for sure. Fortunately, we have friends who might know. Let's ask Travis and Brent, and we can figure out who else might be able to help."

Tyler had the day off, so Seth and Evan drove him and Cameron to Lacey's in time to prep for the breakfast crowd.

"I've got a pre-paid credit card for the video machines and enough small bills for poker and betting," Tyler said. "Should be enough if I dawdle to last all day without people wondering why I'm hanging around."

Evan had spent enough time in rural towns to understand Tyler's caution. He and Cameron had to walk a fine line. Being 'good friends' was one thing, but people could get ugly if they suspected more between them. *Another reason they want to get out of town.*

"People gamble at breakfast?" Evan rarely was awake enough to do his email before coffee, let alone play games of chance for money.

"Folks would play twenty-four-seven if we were open," Cameron said. "And the die-hards go to the big casino in Wheeling, where they can go 'round the clock. I try not to judge. Folks around here don't have much cause for optimism, and the idea of even winning a small amount keeps them going."

He sighed. "I only worry when I hear that someone can't pay their bills because they're spending all their money on the games. It happens. Sometimes a family member will come in to ask us to cut the person off. We can't do that unless the gambler asks us to. Otherwise, they'll just go somewhere else."

Tyler gave him a supportive smile. "Which is another reason to get out of Buckhannon," he said, taking Cameron's hand.

Seth dropped them off at the door. A few minutes later, he and Evan came in and started marking small sigils and runes by the windows and on the doorframe with a Sharpie. Evan knew the symbols wouldn't hold off Swain himself, but they might deter any lieutenants he sent who intended to use lesser magic. They wouldn't stop non-magical henchmen, but Evan hoped they would be reluctant to kidnap Cameron in front of witnesses.

"You've got your charms?" Seth quizzed them. Both men nodded.

"Yes," Cameron said. "We won't go outside until you come back for us. Tyler will stay for my whole shift."

Seth clapped Cameron on the back. "Good. We're going to do our best to wrap this up as soon as we can."

When they went back to the campground, they found a familiar Crown Victoria parked behind the RV. Brent and Travis were walking back from the concession stand with cups of steaming coffee.

"We weren't sure when you'd get back," Travis said, as they traded handshakes and backslaps.

"Come on in. Their coffee is good—but mine is better." Evan murmured the words to open the warding on the RV to admit guests and unlocked the door.

"I told Brent you'd have wardings." Travis lightly slugged his work partner in the shoulder.

"Would they turn a burglar into a toad?" Brent joked.

"Worse." Seth put his keys in a bowl near the door. "Explosive diarrhea. Totally legal, and makes it really hard to escape."

"Cruel but effective," Travis said with a laugh.

Seth ushered them into the RV's living room and turned on the electric fireplace as Evan went to make a fresh pot of coffee.

"Any trouble with the drive?" Seth got mugs and fixings, then grabbed a bag of chocolate chip cookies and brought everything to the table.

"Nah. It's a pretty straight shot except for the last little bit." Travis reached for a cookie. "I forgot how pretty this area is."

"Not to mention how far in the middle of nowhere." Brent helped himself to a cookie as well. "But I did have a vision that might mean something."

Evan looked up. "Oh yeah?"

"I saw a pool of water in a cave," Brent said. "That's it—just a glimpse. I know it isn't much, but I've learned to mention even the little stuff because it usually slots into place at some point."

"Thank you," Seth said. "If it was important enough for you to see, it's something we need to keep in mind."

"And if you think we're in the boonies, we aren't as far out as Swain's Mountain Laurel Lodge." Evan leaned against the kitchen wall. "They're really cut off. At least here, we can use a microwave." Evan brought the pot of coffee when it finished brewing, and they gathered around the table. Seth caught their guests up on everything since the last phone call.

"Brent's friend Drake is planning to meet us at our hotel room later this morning," Travis told them. "We figured we'd order pizza and eat lunch there so we didn't have to worry about being overheard or compromising Drake by being seen in public together."

"We had some thoughts about how to tackle everything and try to beat Swain to the punch," Seth told them as they fixed their coffee. He filled them in on his strategy, and Travis nodded.

"That works," Brent said. "When do you want to go back to the old camp?"

"This afternoon, if Travis is up for it," Evan said. "Swain's already made one attempt on Cameron, and I don't think he'll wait long before he makes another move. With luck, the ghosts can tell us more about where he does his sacrifices. And maybe Travis can help them get peace."

Evan shared the materials Parker sent, and they looked over the map of the lodge compound that he had printed out.

"He sounds like a narcissistic empath." Travis clicked through the website again. "Basically, a Psi-vamp. Other people are just like batteries to them, full of energy they can drain and use. It's not uncommon in celebrities, politicians, and clergy. Most of them are untrained and don't consciously realize that they're doing it. Those who have serious magic and understand what they're capable of doing are the dangerous ones—and I think Swain fits the bill. By the way, you're right. This coffee is better."

Evan's phone chimed, and he glanced down. "Got an email from Parker." He opened the message and took a moment to read it.

"He's found that Swain or his predecessors have had backing from all the bigwigs in town at one point or another. And not just this town —all the way up to the governor. I don't think we're going to get official help on this. We're on our own."

"When we meet up with Drake, show him that list," Brent said. "He can probably validate and fill in the blanks."

They headed out to meet with Drake. Seth and Evan took everything they would need to return to the old camp and followed the Crown Vic to the hotel where Brent and Travis were staying.

The mom-and-pop motor court had a mid-century vibe, although it had clearly been well-maintained through the years. The Mountain Mama Motor Manor had a grinning cartoon bear in a flowered apron on the neon sign. Each door was painted a different vibrant color that matched metal chairs on the walkway out front, and white pierced concrete "breeze stop" partitions added to the 1950s feel.

"Very Route 66," Seth said as they joined Brent and Travis at the door to their room.

"Cheap rates, good Wi-Fi, and free breakfast," Brent replied. "Monster hunting doesn't pay, so we're on a budget."

Just like Seth funded their quest with his security consulting, and Evan's graphic design and photography helped pay the bills, Brent's day job as a private investigator and Travis's non-profit helped keep them in the fight.

The room's décor was a tribute to the outdoor beauty of West Virginia, with vivid scenes of hiking, kayaking, and rock climbing as well as mountain vistas. Two double beds faced a dresser with a large mirror, the bathroom on the left, kitchenette on the right, and a worn Formica-topped table with chairs off to one side.

"I bet you sleep well," Evan quipped, looking at the sporting scenes. "Just thinking about climbing a cliff makes me tired."

Blue painter's tape tacked maps, notes, photos, and printouts to the walls. "Aren't you supposed to have a web of red string crisscrossing all that, like in the movies?" Seth joked.

Brent rolled his eyes and flipped him the bird. "Ran out. You'll just have to use your imagination."

Travis retrieved sodas for everyone and ordered pizza. They had just sat down at the table when Brent's phone rang.

"Yeah, we're in 126," he told the caller. A few minutes later, a knock came at the door. Brent went to answer it but kept his gun at the small of his back.

"Come on in," he welcomed the newcomer. "Everyone, this is Drake Carlson," Brent announced after he shut and locked the door.

Drake was Brent's height, with short-cut, wavy brown hair and dark eyes. Broad shoulders suggested a sports background, while his general bearing screamed "law enforcement."

"Drake—you've talked to Travis on the phone," Brent continued, making introductions. Travis nodded. "Seth and Evan are our friends on Fletcher Swain's tail."

Drake shook hands all around. "Pleased to meet you," he said to Seth and Evan. "Any enemy of Fletcher Swain is a friend of mine."

They sat, four of them around the table, and Brent perched on the corner of the nearest bed. "You've dealt with Swain longer than any of us." Brent looked to Drake. "Do you mind bringing us up to speed?"

"Not at all." Drake leaned back in his chair and crossed his ankle over his knee. "I've been in the Beckley office of the Federal Bureau of Supernatural Investigations for close to two years. I'm a psychic, and I get visions. The FBSI team is small—just me. It's not exactly a friendly environment," he added with a grimace. "A lot of the regular agents don't believe in the supernatural and think I'm making it all up. Half the time, I think my boss agrees with them."

"Sorry to hear that," Brent said. "You deserve better."

Drake gave a rueful smile. "Thanks. Be sure to fill out a comment card." He cracked open the soda can Travis handed him and took a drink.

"My predecessors had a variety of different skills—one was a witch, another was a medium, and someone else was a psychometric. Those are all very different abilities. Just because you can do one thing doesn't mean you can do any of the rest. That's a lesson I keep having to repeat to my boss. I can do what I do well—but I can't do everything."

"You can thank television for the one-size-fits-all occult powers trope," Travis said. "I can sympathize."

"Apparently over the years, the other folks in my role helped to get rid of vengeful ghosts from mine disasters, dispelled curses on mine bosses from pissed-off granny witches, and stopped drug smugglers who used magic to hide what they were doing," Drake went on.

"But after I'd been here for a while, I realized that there were the kinds of cases we looked into—and the ones we didn't. No one had an appetite for looking for missing people, even when there were reasons to think magic or creatures were involved," Drake reported. "That was especially true if the people who went missing had any links to the Summit lodge and Renou-Vous or to Hub, Inc. in Moundsville."

"You say that like those locations had more than their share of disappearances," Seth ventured.

"They did. And going back a ways, so did the land around Camp Morning Glory. So I asked my boss if I could see about closing those cold cases in between situations that needed my help. He shut me down so fast I got whiplash, said those folks were just people who didn't want to be found."

A grin stole across Drake's features. "I rarely take 'no' for an answer. Especially when I can smell bullshit. It seemed real clear that *someone* didn't want those cases looked at, and that just makes my Spidey sense tingle," Drake added.

"I kept digging, off the clock. I found details that didn't make sense, and the way the police and local FBSI handled the situations, it seemed clear to me that they'd been told to either ignore or bury the cases."

"Tell us more," Seth encouraged.

"I grew up in West Virginia. Everyone knows corruption reaches high and runs deep, especially when it comes to protecting the mining companies. But the things I kept stumbling onto—or getting visions about—weren't linked to the mines. They weren't even connected to the main political families in the states, the ones who are guaranteed to never get a speeding ticket and slither out of pretty much everything except maybe shooting someone on live television," Drake said.

"I kept digging, and for the camp and the resort, I found a weird chain of traveling preachers and bogus non-profits who didn't just dodge taxes and flim-flam the flock. People connected to them died or went missing more than normal for anyone who isn't in a cartel or the Mafia."

"And your boss still wouldn't listen?" Seth asked.

Drake shook his head. "By that time, I didn't even try. If he wasn't on the take, he'd been threatened. I promised myself I would figure this out and close it down—and then leave town."

"I'm guessing that Fletcher Swain came up?" Brent ventured.

"More than once. No matter what thread I traced, if I went far enough, there was a connection to Swain. Not just over decades but going back decades under different names. I'd already suspected he was a witch, but the more bodies piled up, I knew there was something seriously bad going on," Drake said.

Cars honked in the parking lot and then raised voices argued, and their conversation stopped amid the noise. Doors slammed, then tires squealed as someone drove away.

"Seth and I have been out to the camp," Evan said, picking up the discussion again. "But what about the resort? Other than that, the holding group that bought it has ties to Swain, and he holds his fancy wellness seminars there."

Travis's phone message chimed, and he went to the door to bring in two large pepperoni pizzas and sodas that had been dropped off. They took a break to dig in, making short work of the food. Brent cleared away the empty boxes, and everyone grabbed new drinks.

Drake took a long sip from his soda. "The Mountain Laurel Lodge has an interesting history, like something out of a horror movie. Several owners were financially ruined because they couldn't make a go of it, more than one murder took place there, and the place has had a legitimate reputation for being haunted since it was built."

"We heard some stories about the haunts from Cameron's boyfriend, who worked there briefly," Seth said. "What did you dig up?"

"The first owner bought the land and built the Mountain Laurel Lodge right after the Second World War—before the Quiet Zone was established," Drake explained. "Since he envisioned a place where people could get away from it all—and given the state of technology back then—the Quiet Zone restrictions didn't make a big difference for him when they were finally implemented."

Drake paused to take a few bites of pizza and wiped the sauce off his lips. "The construction was snakebit from the start. On-the-job injuries when the place was being built, plus at least one death— maybe more that got covered up. Now and then, a worker—and some- times a guest—went missing. Rumors went around that the owner had been a hitman for the Mob and that the ghosts of the people he killed haunted him. Guests claimed to see strange things. Then the owner fell from his balcony and died. It was ruled an accident, but looking at the reports, no real investigation was done. They just wanted to close the case.

"The Mountain Laurel Lodge changed hands a couple of times and tried to re-brand as a family destination and then as a lovers' getaway, but once the Quiet Zone went in, developers got scared off. It sat empty for several years—until the same non-profit that owned Camp Morning Glory bought it and turned it into Summit." Drake paused and returned to the pizza, eating fast like he was famished.

"So real ghosts, some scandals, and the chance to pick up the land at a distressed price," Brent summarized.

"Yep," Drake replied. "Not all that strange for West Virginia, really. Everything's haunted, and there are scandals galore."

Travis leaned forward. "How about the Hub?

"That was definitely on the official 'don't touch' list," Drake said. "So of course..."

"You headed right for it." Brent grinned.

"Am I that predictable?"

"Yes," Brent replied.

"Guilty as charged." Drake didn't look at all remorseful. "Technically, the Hub is a call center and server farm. On the surface, it's squeaky clean. It handles fundraising calls for local charities, political calls for both parties, and emergency messaging for weather alerts."

"But—" Evan prompted.

"Several workers were reported missing by their families and never found. No one in the local police or FBSI seemed overly worried. There have been five confirmed deaths—not counting the missing people— among Hub managers and employees. They are what I'd deem suspicious—one-car accidents, fall from a balcony, drowned alone at a lake —that sort of thing. No apparent witnesses. The families reported the deaths and asked for law enforcement to look into them. The cases were closed almost immediately, with bullshit notes saying there was nothing unusual."

"Yeah, that's not strange at all," Seth muttered.

"Over the last year, we've had an increase in reports of fraud," Drake went on. "Identity theft, impersonation, even deep-fake porn. Before I got transferred here, I worked on money laundering and phishing cases, so whenever a place like the Hub draws attention for one set of possible crimes, I look for the whole enchilada. And then I got told to leave it alone."

"Did they give you a reason?"

Drake snorted. "You mean aside from large campaign contributions to all the right people? No. Gobbledygook about how the Hub is a major employer, important to the tax base, an example of how the state is embracing technology, yada, yada, yada."

Evan could see Drake's frustration and didn't blame the agent. On a much smaller scale, he had dealt with employers who demanded workers turn a blind eye to fraud and theft, and he knew how much it rankled to stand by and do nothing.

"Were any of the things you saw in your visions tied into this stuff?" Evan asked, always curious about how people's abilities worked.

Drake nodded. "I saw faces and matched them to missing persons reports. And then I saw a person change into someone else."

Evan's phone buzzed. He glanced at it and thumbed the notice off. "Just Tyler checking in. So far, nothing unusual."

"How is the Hub connected to Swain?" Seth asked, returning his attention to Drake.

"Through several trusts and shell companies," Drake replied. "Someone definitely wanted to make the link difficult to find."

Seth and Evan exchanged a glance. "Interesting," Seth said. "This isn't the first time we've found the coven members involved in online crime. We helped bust a trafficking and relics theft ring a while ago when we were in South Carolina. I'm not surprised the witch disciples have more than one iron in the fire."

"I know people can do a lot with computers and artificial intelligence to make fake stuff look real," Drake said. "But I think there's even more going on."

"Like what?" Travis asked.

"Doppelgangers. I know it sounds crazy—"

"Not so much," Seth replied.

"I think the Hub is big into cybercrime, but I also think it's connected to other bad shit that's going on," Drake continued, seeming relieved to find people who believed him. "Once I saw the cases about online fraud, I started looking into other complaints. People reported having a person *who looked just like them* show up at the bank and take money out of their account, or sign a lease or hold someone up at gunpoint."

"And you believe them?" Evan's thoughts swirled, coming up with several ways those reports could be true.

"Yes. In each case, the person who supposedly committed the crime had an iron-clad alibi," Drake told them. "Video proof, witnesses—in some cases, people who were at offices where signing in requires biometrics. That was enough to get the case dropped, but it didn't change the fact that *someone* who committed the crimes looked like those people. Which is where I think my vision gives us a clue."

"Was there anything the people who were impersonated had in common?" Evan asked.

"They were all people in local positions of authority," Drake replied. "Even though the cases were dropped, the coverage damaged their reputations, so they had to leave their jobs. It made me wonder if there were other cases that weren't reported because the goal was blackmail."

"Do you have a theory about what really happened?" Seth asked.

Drake glanced to Brent, who gave a nod. "Brent told me that you know about the stuff that isn't supposed to be real. I think that someone recruited shapeshifters for the scams." He tossed out his scenario and looked like he was bracing himself for ridicule.

Evan had seen more than one movie based on the urban legend that lizard people from outer space could impersonate world leaders, even the king of England. Given the present circumstances, those wild scripts didn't seem as funny as before.

"Tyler saw something up at the lodge that sounds a whole lot like a shapeshifter," Seth said. "So your theory isn't as far-fetched as it might seem."

"If someone had a group of creatures who could perfectly impersonate people in positions of power, there's an endless opportunity for chaos," Evan said. "Why stop with blackmail? Just remove the real person and substitute the doppelganger. That would destabilize everything."

"I think you're onto something," Travis cut in. "And shapeshifters aren't the only creatures that can mimic voices or appearance. Crocottas, wendigos, and kitsune can do it. There are ways to catch them, but it requires looking for them in the first place—and that takes believing that creatures like those exist."

Drake sighed in relief. "Thank God, you believe me. There wasn't anyone else I could talk to, no one local I trusted. Then I remembered hearing that Brent survived an attack in the army under some strange conditions, and I reached out."

Evan knew a little about Brent's story. His family and twin brother, Danny, had been slaughtered while he was away at football camp as a teenager, an attack the police chalked up to gang members but which Brent believed to be demonic. During his time in Iraq, his team had been pinned down in a village by supernatural forces, and only Brent's knowledge of how to fight demons and evil spirits based on video games enabled him to save his soldiers. Everyone else died bloody.

"Travis, Seth, and I are going back for another look at the old campground," Evan told Drake. "We think that Swain might have hidden something there that he'll need before he can make the next big move. If we can retrieve it first, that might help save lives."

"Not to mention the restless ghosts and the creepy shadow thing that went after us," Seth said. "We're hoping Travis can help with those."

"In the meantime, I'd like to look closer at the Hub," Brent said. "We might not always play by the rules. Are you in?"

"Following the rules hasn't gotten me anywhere, so yeah, count me in. I'm done with this job and the Bureau after this—although I'd really like to stay out of prison," Drake replied.

Drake and Brent agreed to stay behind and dig deeper into research while Seth, Travis, and Evan headed back to Camp Morning Glory. On the way, Travis called another hacker friend, Teag Logan, whose Weaver magic supercharged his computer skills. Travis recounted the newest updates, including what they had just learned from Drake about the Hub, and Teag promised to have a look.

"How much do you trust Drake?" Evan asked when Travis ended the call.

"Some," Travis admitted. "I haven't fought beside him, so I don't know for sure. That's why I called Teag instead of having Brent do it. No point in admitting to hacking in front of the FBSI," he added with a grin.

"Good thinking," Seth agreed.

Camp Morning Glory looked unchanged. Evan had feared that Swain's henchmen might have swooped in after their visit and somehow gotten rid of the ghosts, but the prickle on the back of his neck confirmed they were still present.

"I see what you mean," Travis said quietly after they passed through the entrance gate.

They had already filled Travis in, both about the ghosts who manifested and the dark presence that chased them away. Travis paused right inside the gate and closed his eyes, confident that Seth and Evan had his back.

"You said this was a church camp? The energy is all wrong." Travis's face was taut with concentration. "The land has been desecrated. So much death."

The air around them felt heavy and oppressive as the temperature plummeted. Evan dropped his bag and hurried to lay down a salt circle around them while Seth loaded rock salt rounds into his shotgun. Travis made a larger circle around them with spray paint, adding symbols that were unfamiliar to Evan. They had expected to get farther into the compound before contacting the spirits, but the ghosts seemed drawn to Travis.

Evan tried not to envision a swarm of ghosts milling around them. He wasn't sure he wanted to know what Travis saw.

Travis opened his eyes. "There are so many of them. Swain used this as his dumping ground long after it was a camp—and even back when it was. It reeks of blood and evil." He sounded like he was waking from a trance.

"If you can get names, we can match them to cold cases and missing person reports," Evan reminded him. "I'll also try to record you."

"Spirits of the camp, show yourselves." Travis's voice was firm, but not commanding. "Tell me your names so we can give closure to those who love you, and I will help you move on."

One by one, ghosts flickered into presence all around them. Evan felt the difference in the energy between the working of a true medium and what he and Seth had attempted. Travis's power felt like an anchor amid the staticky chaos of the spirits, and they gravitated toward his calm.

"Alicia Reston. Lucy Kendall. Kevin Johnson." Travis began a litany of names as Evan scribbled them down in a notebook, not trusting electronic devices to work right amid all the spectral energy.

Seth remained on guard, even while the ghosts kept a respectful distance well back from the salt circle. Although the day had not been cold before, Evan saw his breath in the air, and he started to shiver.

"Kathleen Corcoran. Dennis Smith. Margaret Connor." Travis kept going, a seemingly endless list of names. Evan hurried to keep up as Travis kept a steady cadence, acknowledging the roll call of the dead.

All of these people couldn't have been posse descendants for ritual sacri-fices. Did Swain get addicted to the power boost of between-ritual murders? Were they people who got in the way or asked the wrong questions? Or did he take other liberties and abuse his sway over the flock, then need to clean up his mess by getting rid of witnesses and victims?

Evan sniffed, trying to stop the flow of silent tears. He wiped them away with the back of his hand as they ran cold down his cheeks and dropped onto his tablet. Evan dared a glance at Seth, who remained resolute, but looked pale and shaken.

Some ghosts appeared more solid than others. These were mostly young—teens and twenties. The men Evan figured were the deputies' descendants like him and Seth, the original slate of sacrifices. The women were more numerous, victims of Swain's depravity and evidence that he was above the law and would not incur any penalty for his deeds.

Finally, Travis stopped listing names. They stood surrounded by dozens of ghosts dressed in the clothing of every decade of the past hundred years.

"Tell me your stories," Travis said.

Evan braced himself, but the spirits apparently communicated silently to Travis, or he did not lend them the extra energy to make themselves heard.

The campground grew unnaturally silent, as if even the birds respected the ghosts' confessional. Travis's expression remained stoic, eyes closed, but Evan saw the ex-priest's hands tighten in fists, white-knuckled, and his whole body swayed at times like the stories were a body blow.

Finally, Travis opened his eyes. He had paled and wore an expres-sion of grief and devastation. "We will avenge you. Your loss will not be in vain. Now go in peace and be at rest."

One by one, the spirits winked out of sight. Evan suspected that even more ghosts who remained unseen accepted Travis's invitation and moved on. He stopped the recording and pocketed his phone. Seth passed him another salt-round shotgun.

"The ghosts are gone." Travis's ragged voice and the haunted look in his eyes told Evan that he didn't want to know the details to which Travis had borne witness.

"Thank you," Seth said, and Evan nodded. "Was it Swain's doing?" He handed Travis a bottle of water and a candy bar, which Travis finished off immediately, regaining a bit of his color.

"Yes, Swain was behind the deaths," Travis said, "and I'll tell you more later. But we're not done yet. There's more—"

Evan felt ice slither down his spine, knowing something bad loomed behind them, the same darkness that had chased them from the camp before.

He racked the rounds in his shotgun and patted his pockets, reassuring himself that he had plenty of ammunition. Seth and he took positions on either side of Travis.

"Do what you need to do, Travis," Seth said. "We've got your back."

"Stay inside the painted circle," Travis warned. "What's left isn't ghostly—it's demonic."

Evan had a million questions, but the darkness swept in before he could form the words. He had little magic and no psychic abilities, but primal instinct took over, and his hindbrain screamed for him to run. Forcing himself to stay in place meant ignoring a million years of survival evolution.

The temperature dropped further, with the damp cold of a crypt and the smell of the tomb. Inky blackness engulfed them, blotting out the sun and hiding their surroundings. Hideous screams felt like they pierced his skull, and he gagged from the smell of rot and sulfur.

Seth fired into the void, but the salt didn't affect this manifestation.

Evan raised the high-capacity Super-Soaker filled with salted holy water tinged with colloidal silver.

"Here goes nothing." Evan loosed a powerful stream on the featureless shadow. The demon screeched, nearly deafening him. But the pressure in his mind eased, just a bit, angrier now and still menacing.

Travis raised his voice in the rite of exorcism. "*Exorcizamos te, omnis immundus spiritus...*"

Evan shivered at the power of his words. Travis might have left the church and holy orders long ago, and perhaps his own faith was tattered, but he spoke with the full authority of his ordination.

"*Omnis satanica potestas, omnis incursio…*" Travis continued the litany, clear and strong.

"Keep firing," Seth urged, and Evan fired again, wishing they had brought two of the guns with larger tanks.

Evan thought that the dark entity faded slightly, still hellish and menacing. Despite being protected by the painted circle, Evan sensed the demon's power buffeting at their invisible boundary and felt a wave of devastating grief crash over him.

Everyone we've lost, the ones we couldn't protect, the ones we didn't save, that's all on us, we're responsible. We failed them. We failed—

Evan gritted his teeth and kept on shooting, even though tears ran down his face. He heard Seth sobbing; then he fired round after round into the demon even though the shells didn't seem to hurt the entity.

Travis's voice remained firm. He spoke the ancient Latin smoothly and without pause.

Evan's gun sputtered, spewing the last drops beyond the paint circle. *That's it. I'm done. We're all going to die.*

Travis's voice rose to a crescendo, commanding and clear as he ended the rite. "*Audi nos!*"

The darkness twisted and shrieked, screeching as it tried to breach their protective circle and failed.

The air felt lighter as if a storm had passed, and the temperature rose. After several minutes, birds chirped, and Evan heard the rustle of small animals in the brush.

"What was that?" Seth asked, shaken.

Evan dug a sports drink from his bag and handed it to Travis, who accepted it gratefully, taking several long swallows.

"A grief demon. Brent and I ran into some a while back. They're not common, but they're drawn to places where there have been mass casualties—disaster sites, mine cave-ins, that sort of thing," Travis said.

"They feast on the emotions of the living—and when there aren't people around, they siphon the energy of the dead. In the worst cases, they lure people into their territory to feed off them. I wouldn't be surprised if some of the deaths that happened here were because of that," he added.

Evan had lots of questions about what Travis had learned from the spirits, but right now he couldn't wait to put the abandoned camp in the rearview mirror. Seth kept the shotgun ready as Evan helped Travis pack his gear, and Evan kept his gun handy while they walked back to the truck.

"Do you think the demon will return?" he asked after they were back on the main road.

Travis shook his head. "I doubt it. The ghosts have moved on, and people have no reason to visit the site. That removes the food source, and being exorcised usually dissipates a particular demon for the foreseeable future."

"What did the ghosts tell you?" Seth asked, beating Evan to the punch.

Travis finished his bottle of water and leaned back against the headrest. "Their names—if they could remember—and how they died. Some had been dead long enough that they were fading. There were a few true accidents—falls, a drowning, a sudden illness. But all the rest were killed by Swain. They were either murdered elsewhere and the bodies dumped at the camp, or they died at the camp, and the cause of death was covered up. So many…" His voice drifted off.

"I saw mostly women. Were the men and boys the ritual sacrifices?" Evan asked.

Travis nodded. "They were from before Swain re-opened the resort and changed the name to Summit. The last several cycles—like with Cameron's father—didn't happen here. Their bodies are probably on the mountain."

"Thank you," Seth replied. "Did you get any strong sense for something that might be Swain's anchor relic?"

"No. I didn't pick up on anything else paranormal beyond the ghosts and the demon. If Swain is using a different location for his rituals, it stands to reason he'd keep his anchor close at hand," Travis said.

They drove back to the hotel where Travis and Brent were staying. Drake's car was gone.

"Want to come in? We can find out what Brent's been doing while we were risking life and limb." Travis still looked a little shaky.

Seth shook his head, and Evan felt certain that Seth shared his concern that Travis needed a chance to rest and recover.

"We'll check back with you later after we've made sure Cameron and Tyler are okay," Seth assured Travis. "And I want to talk with Teag about some 'computer research.'"

"Let us know how that goes. Talk to you soon." Travis climbed out of the truck's cab.

They waited until Travis had gone inside and gave the lot a careful once-over to assure themselves no one was watching the room before they pulled away.

"That was...pretty damn terrifying," Seth admitted.

"Yeah. But Travis thinks it worked—and all those souls are at rest. When this is done, someone's going to need to make an anonymous tip about the bodies," Evan pointed out.

"Once we take Swain out of the picture, maybe the local cops will give a damn."

They drove to Lacey's. The lot was nearly full, and Evan realized the dinner crowd and evening gamblers were probably filtering in. Seth parked next to Cameron's SUV, and they headed inside.

Tyler sat at the end of the bar, nursing a Coke. He leaned into the corner so he had a view of the whole room, even if he was ostensibly watching a game he'd probably bet on. Seth and Evan took seats next to him, and Cameron gave them a nod in acknowledgment.

"How did today go?" Evan asked.

"Good, I guess. As in, not bad. No one tried anything, and I've kept a lookout on the people who came and went. Didn't see anyone who seemed creepy or paid too much attention to Cam," Tyler reported, dropping his voice.

Evan dug into his pocket and handed Tyler a silver medallion. "Wear this—and make sure Cameron wears that St. Michael's charm his mother gave him. Some of the creatures involved can take the shape of other people, but they can't wear silver," he said in a voice just above a whisper.

Tyler dropped the chain over his head. "I'll check with Cam, but he never takes off that necklace from his mom." He looked around to make sure no one was close enough to hear them. "Shapeshifters? You're sure?"

Evan nodded. "We can tell you more when we're somewhere private. For now, just stay close to Cam and watch his back."

"Do you need a break? We were going to order dinner," Seth offered.

"I'd be happy for the company, but I planned to stay until the end of Cam's shift and take him home," Tyler said. "I have to work tomorrow, so I'll need someone to cover for me until I can get back here."

"I've got it," Seth said. "I can work on my computer from here as well as anywhere."

Evan got up to use the bathroom and paused beside the community bulletin board in the back hallway. A flier caught his eye.

Ready for a fresh start? Want to leave the past behind and create a new you? Renou-Vous at the Summit Lodge can help. Come to our free, no-obligation information meeting and find out more!

The colorful poster included the address for the local library with a date and time that Evan realized was tomorrow.

He checked to make sure no one saw him unpin the paper and tuck it into his pocket. When he returned to the bar, Seth had already put in their burger order and gotten sodas for them. Evan showed the advertisement to Tyler and Seth.

"I have an idea—"

Seth fixed him with a glare. "Absolutely not."

Evan raised his chin. "You don't even know what I was going to say."

"No, but I know *you*."

Evan laid out his plan to attend the meeting, and Seth looked daggers at him.

"That's way too dangerous," Seth protested.

Evan rolled his eyes. "I'll wear a wire. You can hear everything. Travis and Brent could be on the outside in case I need help. I won't go anywhere else with anyone. But we might get an idea of how they get people suckered in."

The tic in Seth's jaw gave Evan an idea of how little his partner liked the idea. "And you don't think it's convenient that the meeting is happening now, once we're in town? It's a trap."

Evan shrugged. "Maybe. But we're going to have to go up to the lodge, and it would help to know more."

"This isn't just because you're in town." Tyler glanced at the poster. "Those have been up for months. I don't know if anyone ever goes to the meetings, but they hold one every week."

"Have you heard any gossip about them? Do you know someone who went?" Seth asked.

"More importantly—does anyone who went ever come back?" Evan put in.

"I don't know," Tyler admitted. "No one I've talked to ever said anything about going."

They paused as Cameron served their food. "That guy on the third game machine keeps looking back this way," he warned in a low tone. "Might be nothing, but it seems strange to me."

Evan glanced over his shoulder, but the gambler had his back to them. "I'm watching him," Tyler assured them. "I thought at first he was glancing at the TVs, but now I'm sure he's keeping an eye on Cam."

The burgers were better than Evan expected, maybe because people who came to bet also appreciated good food. For a weeknight, the bar had steady business. Not everyone came to gamble, but the poker tables filled up fast, and most of the folks there for a drink or a bite to eat stopped at the machines for a game or two. One of the players never moved, raising a flag to indicate that he wanted to order and eat where he was.

"He's pretty hardcore," Evan observed.

"That's Bill." Cameron refilled their sodas as he spoke. "His wife died six months ago and his dog passed away shortly afterward; the kids all live out of state, and he's got bad arthritis. Bill plays low stakes all day, but he says it gets him out of the house, and he has a budget."

Cameron's shift ended at six. Tyler, Seth, and Evan waited to walk out with him. The man who had been looking in their direction was gone.

Evan spotted him having a smoke near the dumpsters behind the bar, along with a second man. They looked up when Evan and the others walked their direction, but when they saw Cameron surrounded by three bodyguards in security formation, they pretended to turn away and focus on their smokes.

"Do you know them?" Seth asked Cameron.

"The guy who was in the bar has been around for the last week or so. Haven't seen the other one," Cameron replied.

Seth and Evan made sure Cameron and Tyler were in their SUV with the doors locked before getting into the truck. They followed the CR-V from the lot and stayed right behind them until they reached Cameron's house

"Better safe than sorry," Seth said by way of apology as he and Evan followed the two men inside, staying long enough to check the protections and ensure that no one had tampered with the locks.

"I'll pick you up first thing and head over to the bar," Seth promised Cameron. "Maybe I'll get lucky at poker again."

They said goodnight and headed for the RV. Evan's phone buzzed with a text.

"It's Parker. He says he just emailed me info linking Lacey's to a holding company of Swain's. Parker thinks it's money laundering," Evan reported.

"I suspect Swain's got his hooks into the whole town by now." Seth was silent for a moment. "Are you sure you want to go to that meeting tomorrow?"

Evan picked up on his partner's worry and loved him for it. But they both knew they came here with a job to do.

"I'll be careful. I won't take any chances or go off script. Won't eat or drink anything they offer or be out of sight of the group. You'll have the audio feed, and Travis can be backup. Maybe we'll learn something that will give us an edge."

"I love you. Don't do anything stupid," Seth grumbled.

"You're cute when you're brooding and protective." Evan leaned in to steal a kiss. "It'll be okay."

Please, let it be okay.

6

SETH

"YOU'RE VERGING ON 'COMIC BOOK VILLAIN LAIR' WITH THAT SETUP," Evan joked when he looked at how Seth had transformed the RV's living room.

Seth's main computer console was on the table, but he had three other screens set up and co-opted the TV as well. Lines of code scrolled down the monitors, which occasionally blinked and beeped, reminding Seth of the gambling machines at Lacey's. He did not overlook the irony.

"Brent, Teag, and I are all worming our way inside the Hub." Seth paused to take a sip of coffee from his giant mug. "We each took a different line of attack, looking for specific information and system weaknesses."

"So glad you use your superpower for good instead of evil." Evan leaned against the counter with his coffee and a muffin. "What are you hoping to find?"

Seth held up a finger for Evan to wait when a monitor to his left chimed. He glanced at the screen for a second and then hit a key for the program to continue.

"Nothing fancy—for now. We want to figure out what data is being collected and for whom, and what's being done with that data, for starters," Seth replied.

"Teag's going after the ensorcelled encryption. Any of the data and feeds with that level of security are probably high value. Brent's looking for evidence of money laundering, trafficking, and cybercrime. I'm looking for links to the remaining witch disciples and tracing Renou-Vous data, plus anything that might be blackmail-worthy," Seth said.

"Are you going to shut it down?"

"Depends on what we find, but probably," Seth answered. "Not until we've harvested enough evidence against Swain and his cronies to sway law enforcement that aren't on his payroll. Then a nice denial-of-service attack and a few targeted malware injections should bring it to a screeching halt."

"And you're making sure Drake doesn't know about any of this? I'd hate to stop Swain and end up on federal charges," Evan remarked.

"Drake is going undercover unofficially to check out the Hub itself." Seth leaned back and cradled his coffee. "I think he'll quit the FBSI once we bring Swain to account. He's burned out and disillusioned. Between you and me, I wouldn't be surprised if he ends up working with Brent's PI agency, at least for a while. He could be a real asset with his skills, and he already believes in the supernatural."

"If he doesn't like cold weather, Teag could probably find a use for him down in South Carolina."

"It's plenty cold here—I'm not sure Pittsburgh would be worse." Seth hurried to check another screen after a tell-tale sound alerted him. That brought a smile as he checked the results and touched another key.

"These will run all day, maybe into the night. The Hub is huge. We're all mapping a piece of it. Some clients appear to be legit. If possible, we'll leave their data alone. Whether we can do that depends on how the system is set up. If it's too interconnected, then there might not be a choice except to freeze the whole thing," Seth said.

"Anything yet?"

"I've already found files on local movers and shakers who are clearly blackmail material. Some senior people in the FBI and FBSI as well," Seth told him. "I think the photos and videos were made with doppelgangers. So we know who we can't trust because they're already compromised."

"What about the other witch disciples?"

"I'm documenting links, and I think we'll find more, especially with Brent digging into the money trail. The warlocks might not like or trust each other, but they've had to collaborate in order to survive," Seth replied. "They've built out their illegal revenue streams like a Mafia empire, and if Swain's Hub has been their online clearinghouse and record keeper, we might be able to shut them down for good."

"Can you still monitor me wearing a wire at the meeting?"

Seth knew better than to argue with Evan about attending the event, but he heard a tinge of concern in his partner's tone.

"Of course. I'll run that through my phone. It'll be live the whole time, so I'll hear and record what you hear," Seth assured him. "I've got an earpiece for you that just looks like a regular Bluetooth, but you'll be able to talk to me. And you'll have Travis for backup."

"Don't you need to be at Lacey's to watch over Cameron?"

Seth grinned. "All these babies roll up to my laptop, so I can monitor them in real time while I work on something completely legal and boring as I'm holding down a table at the bar."

Seth finished his coffee and then packed up his laptop and the backpack that would let him spend the day at Lacey's. He folded Evan into a hug and squeezed tight.

"Be careful." Seth kissed Evan deep and slow. "There's always more than one way to get information. Don't put yourself in danger. If things go sideways, just say 'Allegheny,' and I'll send Travis in, guns blazing."

Evan returned the kiss and ran his fingertips down Seth's cheek. "Thank you for worrying about me. I'll be careful, and I'll safeword out if there's a problem. Watch your back at the bar. We know they're watching Cameron, and sooner or later Swain is going to get impatient about us being in the way."

Seth gave him one final peck on the lips. "I will. Come back safe." He punctuated his comment with a squeeze and playful slap to Evan's ass.

He left the other computers running as he and Evan locked up and warded the RV. Evan swung by Cameron's house to pick him up and then dropped Seth and Cameron off at Lacey's. He waited until they were inside to drive away, saying that he wanted to hole up at the coffee shop across from the library to see who showed up to the Renou-Vous event early.

Seth tried to ignore the worried pang he felt watching the taillights disappear. "Anything I can do to help you get the day started?" he asked Cameron, sounding more gruff than usual.

"Not really. I've got it down to a science by now," Cameron replied. "I don't unlock the door until we officially open—security and insurance reasons—so if an early bird knocks, don't answer. Grab the table you want and get comfy. I'll get the coffee started."

Seth set his bag down at a table that let him watch the room, then insisted on making the rounds with Cameron to check the back door, lend a hand, and be a protective presence as they brought in deliveries.

He came back to the table and set up his laptop, tying into the feeds that were running back at the trailer. Those windows were too small for anyone to see important information if they happened to glance at his screen but kept Seth clued into the progress.

A rap on the door made Seth look up. Cameron was busy in the back, and Seth remembered his warning. Seth drew his gun but kept it low by his leg and went to look out the front window.

The man who had been watching Cameron on the previous day waited impatiently outside.

"Not open yet," Seth called through the window.

"Then why are you inside?" the man yelled back.

"I'm Security," Seth said with a shit-eating grin.

The man's expression made it clear he didn't like being denied entry, or maybe he was pissed off that Cameron wasn't a sitting duck working alone before the kitchen crew showed up. His scowl didn't faze Seth, and when the guy figured out he couldn't intimidate his way inside he flipped Seth off and retreated to his car.

"What's up?" Cameron came out of the kitchen with a tray of muffins for the glass domes on the bar to feed the early birds. The smell of coffee and bacon filled the bar.

"Stalker-guy is annoyed that I won't let him in early."

"Good for him," Cameron replied. "The kitchen crew showed up. I told them that we had some sketchy types hanging around, so they're both packing heat."

"Probably wouldn't hurt to get medallions for them too," Seth mused.

"Beat you to it. Kenny saw mine and asked about it, then he and Bobby showed me the ones their mamas got them. Real silver. I didn't give them the whole story, but they've got protection," Cameron said.

"Thanks for checking." Seth glanced at his phone. Evan's meeting at the library wasn't until lunch, so he had some time before he needed to listen in.

Seth knew that Evan had come a long way since their early days together. Back then, Seth had been fully responsible for protecting his new partner as Evan learned about weapons and rote magic and delved deep into the supernatural. But Evan was smart and diligent, a quick learner. He could take care of himself in most circumstances. Now, he and Evan watched out for each other, equals on the hunt as well as in the other aspects of their relationship.

That's how it should be.

Much as Seth believed in the concept, his protective streak balked at letting Evan take risks, especially if he wasn't right there to back him up.

Falling in love had surprised Seth with the intensity of his feelings. He had looked out for his army comrades while they were deployed. Seth had tried to protect his brother Jesse and would never forgive himself for failing. He knew that the powerful need to keep Evan safe sprang from that failure, and he tried to keep his impulses in check. And yet...

Seth couldn't shake his discomfort. The plan to attend the meeting made sense. Evan had Travis to back him up, and Seth would be listening the whole time. But they were up against old and powerful witches, and while they had learned ways to defend themselves, neither they nor their friends could face down Swain head-on.

When we're done, none of the deputies' descendants ever have to worry again. It will all be over.

But I'd walk away today without completing the mission if it was the only way to save Evan.

Nothing, not even avenging Jesse, is worth losing him.

While he was in Lacey's, Seth kept his online searches to publicly available data—still a treasure trove of information for someone who knew where to look and how to piece a picture together. He started with the deeds and licenses for the Mountain Laurel Lodge, compiling a list of local and state officials whose favor had to be curried to get the permissions necessary to renovate the old resort into Summit. Other record searches yielded names of people involved as speakers or supporters. Seth suspected that once they parsed through the Hub data, he'd be able to follow the money and see who was paid for their influence.

He went through the information Parker had already supplied on Swain's Renou-Vous wellness seminars, frustrated that what he found was suspicious, but not illegal. Seth knew they would have to pay a visit to the resort, but he wanted to have good intel before taking that risk.

He didn't let himself get too engrossed since he was still on guard duty for Cameron. By now, Seth recognized the regulars. Some came for breakfast and stayed all day, while others drifted in just before lunch or mid-afternoon and played late into the evening. They acknowledged each other with a tip of the head or a one-word greeting, but the nature of gambling made them competitors instead of colleagues, and so they remained solitary.

The guy who seemed to be keeping an eye on Cameron came back shortly after the bar opened, and now apparently included Seth in his surveillance. He left late in the morning, but Seth suspected he hadn't gone far.

Cameron served them all with an easy smile and natural charm that made even the gruffest patron soften a little. Whether he was slinging coffee or mixing drinks, he managed to be efficient while not seeming too busy to interact with customers. That was a real gift, and Seth hoped Cameron could do better for himself once he and Tyler got out of Buckhannon.

His phone rang, and Seth recognized Brent's number. "Hey, I can listen more than I can talk," he said quietly, adjusting his earbuds. "What's up?"

"Drake got in and out," Brent reported. "He can give you the whole story himself when we get back together. What he saw corroborates our theories, and so does what's coming up on my 'search.'"

Given his responsibility to protect Cameron and monitor Evan's covert activity, Seth had only been watching the screen feeds to make sure nothing got hung up, not reading the data. "I'll have to look closely when I get home, but mine's still running."

"Travis told me about Evan's 'outing.' I'm on speed dial if they need more backup. Don't worry."

"Who said I was worrying?"

Brent chuckled. "You remind me of how my father fusses over my mother to take her pills, drink water, and remember her doctors' appointments. It's adorable."

"Did you just call us an old married couple?" Seth couldn't decide whether to be amused or annoyed.

"If it fits—"

"Thanks for helping Travis watch out for Evan. I appreciate it."

"Goes with the territory. That's what friends are for."

The call ended, and Seth's phone chimed softly, reminding him that it was time to monitor Evan's visit to the Renou-Vous meeting.

"Can you hear me?" Evan's voice sounded in Seth's earbud.

"Loud and clear," Seth replied. "Can you see Travis?"

"Yeah, he's sitting on a bench at the front of the library, reading a book," Evan replied. "That'll give him a good view of everyone who comes and goes."

"You remember the drill?"

Evan gave an audible sigh. "Yes. It'll be okay. I've got my medallions, loose salt in my pockets, a silver shiv in my shoe, and one of those protective mojo bags from Teag's friend. I've also got my wooden rune disks, just in case. I won't eat or drink, I'll sit with a clear view of the door, and I promise not to go anywhere with anyone."

Evan's rote magic worked better with sigils, so he carried a piece of chalk and kept wooden "coins" marked with the most common symbols that activated his spells for times when circumstances wouldn't allow him to draw the runes.

"I just worry."

"I know."

He heard Evan draw a deep breath. "I'd better go in. See you on the other side."

Seth heard clothing rustle, the squeak of a door opening and closing, and muted voices through the link. He fought the compulsion to call Travis and check in.

They both know what they're doing.

Seth forced himself to play solitaire on his laptop while he listened.

"Welcome! We're always glad to see new faces. I'm Josh, and I'll be one of the guides for today," a man's voice said. He sounded thirty-ish.

"I'm Sonny." Evan fell back on the alias he used when he and Seth first met and he was dodging a stalker ex-boyfriend in Richmond.

"Come on in, Sonny," Josh said. "We have some bottled water and bags of cookies if you want a snack. We'll get started in a few minutes, but please wander around, meet the other folks and our staff, and have a look at the displays. I hope you'll like what you see and hear today."

Seth gritted his teeth. He knew he was cynical to distrust someone just because they were perky and friendly, but knowing that Swain was involved with the wellness resort gave him good reason.

Other voices carried over the wire, a mix of women and men, mostly pleasantries and chitchat. Evan had been a bartender and a restaurant server, so his skill with small talk exceeded Seth's abilities and patience. While Evan had learned to fight, he also lacked the indelible mark of military service that showed in Seth's stance and movements.

That makes him the better shill for this. He doesn't look dangerous. Seth realized that he was clenching his fist under the table.

"The campus looks very nice," Evan remarked. "Was the main building the original lodge? Does everyone stay there, or are the side buildings for attendees?"

Seth realized that Evan's questions and remarks were narrating his surroundings.

"The lodge has been fully restored to a mid-century modern retro vibe," a woman replied. "We call it 'kitschy-cool.' You'll be happy to know that the spa treatments and the food are thoroughly modern."

"Do people come and go to attend classes, or do they live there for a while?" Evan pressed.

"It depends," the woman answered. "We have some who come for the one-week and two-week programs. Others choose to stay longer, and a few advanced students take advantage of our residency program."

"I have to admit, this whole 'wellness' thing is new for me." Evan managed to sound bashful. "But I like the idea of getting away from all the stress I have going on."

"Exactly! And our teachers have techniques you can use when you go home that keep the stress down to a dull roar," his contact replied.

"Is it true that you can't use cellphones or microwaves?" Evan asked.

The woman laughed. "There are restrictions, but we're not totally cut off from civilization. The strict rules are only right around the observatory. But we lean into leaving those distractions behind."

"I can get a little claustrophobic," Evan lied. "It looks like there's only one road in. Have you ever had problems with flooding or rockslides?"

"Not that I've heard." She sounded amused but slightly guarded. "We take every precaution to ensure our guests are safe and happy. Despite the Quiet Zone, emergency services have exemptions. Being 'cut off' is more a state of mind than a reality."

Seth wasn't sure he believed that, but she made a good pitch.

"Do you have anything in particular that makes you anxious?" The woman asked Evan. "By the way, I'm Jennifer."

"My boyfriend's a first responder," Evan said. "It's a dangerous job. I worry about him a lot, but he's good at it and he gets a lot of satisfaction from the work."

Seth suddenly had the feeling that Evan wasn't just making up responses.

"And how about your work?"

They had talked about making sure Evan remained untraceable, and this wasn't the first time they had infiltrated somewhere with a false persona. As a former bartender, Evan was good at being personable without getting too personal. Still, hearing him talk to the woman gave Seth an unsettled feeling.

Is he unhappy? Has the "quest" gotten to be too much? Am I turning into one of those obsessed bastards like in the movies?

"I'm a freelance photographer," Evan told her, which was partially true. "You know how it is—lots of freedom, no steady paycheck. It's nice for now, but I don't think I want to be doing this for the rest of my life."

Between Seth's online security work, Evan's growing graphic design business—and the low costs of their RV lifestyle—money wasn't an issue. Still, Seth had thought about what it would take to settle down when the coven was destroyed.

Buy a house. Go on vacations. Put some aside for retirement. Live to old age.

We need to talk. I don't want to assume we're on the same page. What if he wants something different?

"Better take your seat—the program's starting," Jennifer told Evan.

"You've got a good turnout," Evan remarked. "Probably thirty people—and four of your team. Is it always this busy?"

"I think it's a sign of the times," she replied. "People are searching for peace. We try to help them find a way to forget all their worries."

Seth shivered. While the woman's delivery made the words sound reassuring, knowing Swain's involvement and the fate of his victims gave them an entirely different meaning.

"I guess I can see the appeal—I mean, if you didn't have other attachments," Evan said. "Or if you were feeling adrift."

Seth wasn't sure whether Evan was playing his role or if there was a hint of something deeper in his wistful tone. *We are so going to talk.*

"Exactly," Jennifer agreed. "When you're part of Renou-Vous, you're family."

Seth knew that many cults and unhealthy wellness groups made the same pitch to people who felt alone. The combination of friendly representatives and the promise of a place to belong was powerful. At the lowest point in his life, he might have felt the pull himself.

"Go ahead and sit down," she repeated. "We're about to get started."

Seth heard rustling as Evan probably inched across a row of seats. "I hope this isn't a slide show," Evan said for Seth's benefit, probably voiced to the person sitting next to him.

"Did you have a look around? What did you think—" Evan went on, clearly talking to someone at the event.

Evan's voice cut out, and the link went dead.

7

EVAN

EVAN TRIED TO PLAY IT COOL EVEN THOUGH HIS HEART RACED. HE DREW on his experience as a bartender, chitchatting with strangers and watching every little detail. When he answered the questions of the overly friendly lodge staff, he tried to make sure he conveyed information to Seth and hoped this whole outing would be useful.

Knowing that Seth could hear everything eased his stress. Seeing Travis outside helped too. Evan knew that if push came to shove, he wasn't exactly helpless on his own, but he preferred not to test his luck.

Evan also had the auris charm to help protect him against lies and manipulation, which made him more confident. And he had wooden sigil disks in his pocket to channel his own minor magic quickly.

The event filled the library's community room. Colorful displays on tables along the walls showed photos of the lodge buildings and interiors. If the place really looked as good as the pictures, someone had put serious money into bringing the abandoned Mountain Laurel Lodge back from oblivion and turning it into Swain's Summit.

One of the things Evan noticed immediately was a symbol that hadn't been on the flier but was everywhere on the posters and materials—a heraldic shield with two crossed keys behind it. He committed the symbol to memory and vowed to find out more when the meeting was over.

Evan mumbled about the photos as if he was talking to himself. "They've got an outdoor pool and a spa in what looks to be a natural cave underneath the building. Big dining room, large gathering hall… some of the sleeping rooms are in the main lodge, and the rest are in outbuildings. Looks nice."

A cave with a pool? Like in Drake's vision? That can't be a coincidence.

He had hidden his phone so it couldn't be taken away, but that kept him from snapping photos. Evan looked for likely places Swain might have hidden his anchor or where he could possibly do his ritual but didn't expect to find them on the public map.

There are a lot of woods around the resort. I wonder if any old outbuildings exist from the lodge's past. Maybe a few caves or old mine entrances? If Swain wasn't using the camp anymore, then everything has to be close to the lodge.

Evan did his best to look engaged and interested while analyzing everything he saw. The four "guides" all looked to be in their early thirties. Their "business casual" style walked a line between looking professional and remaining casual enough to sell the Renou-Vous experience as relaxing.

Despite the friendly greeting, Evan tried not to fidget. Intuition told him something wasn't right, and he had learned the hard way to trust his gut. Despite his protests to Seth, he wished his partner was beside him.

Evan tried to figure out what made him jumpy. Given the room full of people, he wasn't worried about physical danger. Staying away from eating and drinking ruled out getting drugged, and he doubted Swain intended to use sleeping gas on the whole library to kidnap them.

Maybe my bullshit meter is just finely tuned to being manipulated. God knows enough people in my past tried.

Like in any sales presentation, the cheerful friendliness was insincere. As they took their seats, Evan sized up the other attendees. They ranged in age from thirties to fifties, with most falling toward the younger end of the range. Most were trim and looked like they probably favored yoga or running over lifting weights. Although price hadn't been discussed, the crowd looked reasonably well-off.

Evan didn't expect Swain to make an appearance since the witch disciple's picture didn't appear anywhere in the resort materials. Two guides ushered a distinguished-looking man in a linen shirt and loose slacks into the room and toward the podium.

"Everything okay? You stopped talking—" Seth's voice cut off mid-sentence.

Evan didn't dare check his connection, trusting that his hidden phone would continue to record even if something disrupted the wire he wore. He wondered if someone had used a signal-dampening device to ensure confidentiality, although so far, the event had hardly been worthy of top-secret handling.

He took a deep breath to calm himself. *Seth knows where I am. Travis is just outside. We're still in a public library. Seth doesn't need to storm the gates armed to the teeth, and Travis doesn't need to raise an army of the dead. No one else here has probably even realized the cell signal dropped.* He let his hand curl around the magic-dampening charm he wore and felt glad that the auris talisman protected him from being manipulated.

"Welcome. I'm pleased to see so many smiling faces," the older man greeted the crowd. "I'm Paul Wellington, one of the mentors for Renou-Vous. Thank you for coming. I'll make this short so you have time to look at the materials and ask questions of our guides.

"Summit Lodge and the Renou-Vous seminar program are different from the other spas and retreat centers you might have encountered," he continued. "We're not as luxurious as some, although visitors will confirm that the rooms are comfortable and the food is amazing. We aren't in a prestigious location, although the mountain views in the morning are second to none. But what we can offer you is magic."

Evan's ears pricked up at that. Some in the audience smiled at the word, while others appeared to remain hopefully skeptical. Only Evan knew how true that statement might be.

Does Swain bewitch them to take their energy and give them some sort of euphoria? Maybe he uses his abilities to make sure they don't notice anything strange.

"You'll feel better than ever, sleep well, get your appetite back if it's been missing—and more," the man promised. "Follow the program while you're a guest, and it will change your life. You won't just be rested—you'll be *renewed.*"

The speaker left the stage to scattered applause, and the woman who had greeted Evan took his place. "It's hard to follow that, but we'll do our best. Come get some refreshments, look at the posters, and ask plenty of questions. And if you're ready to make the best decision of your life, we are booking reservations for all programs—including our overnight introductory session."

To Evan's surprise, no one made a beeline to the door. His hand went to the deflection necklace at his throat, and he wondered if a hex bag or spell on the room increased audience receptiveness.

Watching the others speak with the guides, Evan thought the ones who were most engaged seemed a little lost. He remembered what it had been like before Richmond, when he had fled an abusive boyfriend and been disowned by his family, bouncing from one temporary gig to another until he had gotten the job at Treddy's bar, where his co-workers made him feel like he belonged.

Now that he and Seth were together, he had a partnership and a purpose. They had friends like Travis and Brent. Sometimes Evan felt exhausted, and there were moments of sheer terror, but now that he had a found family, he never felt alone.

That's how Swain and his shills suck in the most vulnerable people. They're promising peace and community. It's compelling, and people who are desperate and lonely won't look too hard at the details. They might also not be noticed quickly if they vanish.

Evan knew that Seth would be beside himself with the signal cut off. It surprised him that Travis hadn't broken down the door already.

In a burst of madness or inspiration, Evan took one of the forms. "Is there still room on the one-night orientation?" he asked Jennifer.

She grinned like he had given her a puppy. "Are you thinking of joining us? We have another overnight starting tomorrow. We'd love to have you come look around and see the lodge. I'm sure once you do, you'll want to come back for a longer session."

Evan filled in the form before he had time to second-guess himself and tried not to think about Seth's reaction.

"How does this work?"

"You can drive to the Summit, or we run a shuttle bus from the library," Jennifer told him. "All you need is an overnight bag. The one-day orientation is very reasonably priced at one hundred dollars. Meals are included. There's even a spa preview that you won't want to miss."

"I can't wait." Although the butterflies in Evan's stomach made him want to throw up. "Can I take another form? I have a friend who might want to sign up."

"Sure." Jennifer handed him the paper. "My email is at the bottom of the page—just let me know if we'll have one more joining us."

He started to leave and then paused. "What is the symbol that's on all the materials?" He pointed to a heraldic shield with two crossed keys behind it.

"That's the crest of Renou-Vous's founder, Fletcher Swain," Jennifer said. "It's been in his family for generations. You'll see it around the lodge as well."

I might have just gotten a clue about Swain's anchor. "Family crest," *my ass.*

Evan picked up a brochure and tucked it into his pocket.

"Are you sure you don't have any other questions?" Jennifer asked.

"What are the costs like for the longer programs?" Evan felt like she was trying to stall him, and he didn't want to lag behind the others, who had begun to leave.

"We make sure that cost is never a problem," Jennifer assured him. "We have payment plans and financing, and even scholarships. There are plans for every budget. If that's what's keeping you from signing up for other programs, please don't worry."

Evan thought he heard desperation beneath her pleasant tone. He was used to dodging sales pitches for everything from cell phone plans to used cars, but something about Jennifer's voice made him hesitate.

Does she get in trouble if she doesn't meet her quota of signups? Maybe she's worried about more than getting a bonus.

"How long have you been involved with Renou-vous?" He knew he couldn't delay much longer without the cavalry coming in to rescue him.

"Two years." Jennifer's relief that Evan hadn't left yet was palpable —and suspicious.

"How did you get involved?"

Her smile faltered. "I was coping with a tragedy. My sister disappeared, and I ran myself ragged looking for answers. Then I found Renou-vous and realized that it's possible to be at peace even when there are no answers."

Evan studied her expression. Her voice sounded sincere, and her eyes begged him to believe her, but something in her body language seemed at odds, and he wondered if the guides themselves were under a geas.

"Thank you for your time." Evan really hoped that his leaving wouldn't cause trouble for her. "I need to get back to work. People are waiting for me. See you tomorrow."

Before she could protest, Evan slipped out the doors and into the main library. He pulled harder than necessary, expecting them to be spelled shut, and nearly stumbled backward when they opened normally.

Despite the session going over its allotted time and lunch hour being over, no one followed him out, which made him wonder again about some sort of compulsion spell.

He was not surprised to find Travis seated where he had a view of the doors. They exchanged a glance, and Travis gave a nod in acknowledgment.

As soon as he was outside the meeting room, his phone vibrated with missed messages.

"Seth?" he murmured, wondering if the wire was transmitting again.

"Evan? Are you okay? Travis moved into position—"

"I'm fine," Evan said. "I'll tell you all about it once I have a chance to sort what I saw. Travis is right here, and I'm heading back to meet you at Lacey's."

He accepted Seth's grunt as confirmation, knowing his partner was probably still letting go of his worry. Travis rose and followed him, catching up to Evan in the parking lot.

"Thanks for keeping an eye on things." Evan glanced around to make sure none of the lodge people were nearby.

"I'm curious to hear what went on inside. I sent a ghost in when your link went down, but I don't think I got the full story," Travis replied.

"I wondered if there was some sort of spell going on," Evan said. "I'll be glad to debrief you and Brent, and I want to hear your thoughts."

"Go assure Seth that you're safe, and we'll catch up with you later." Travis grinned.

EVAN DROVE BACK TO THE BAR, TRYING TO SORT THROUGH HIS IMPRESSIONS of the event. On the surface, it had been an unremarkable sales pitch— not as compelling as some of the timeshare meetings he had gone to for the free lunch.

But on another level, Evan knew there was more going on. Multiple spells, perhaps to keep people present and receptive. He also realized that despite paying close attention and planning to report back on what he heard, the more time that passed since he left the meeting, the dimmer the memory became.

Maybe they don't want the details well-known for a variety of reasons. So the memories fade to vague impressions.

More magic—and manipulation. Swain is definitely up to no good.

Seth looked relieved when Evan walked through the door to Lacey's. He gave Evan a once-over, and Evan smiled and nodded in reassurance, walking directly to his table.

"I'm fine," Evan said. "And I'm hoping my phone recorded the rest of the presentation after the wire cut out."

"Travis knew you hadn't gone anywhere, and his ghosts kept an eye on you." Seth sounded gruff, and Evan knew his partner was covering his worry.

"Yeah, he told me that. There was definitely some magic happening on several levels." He started to tell Seth about the meeting, but Seth stopped him with a touch to the back of his hand.

"What you told that woman…about worrying over your 'first-responder' partner and feeling anxious about your 'freelance.' Did you mean that? Do you really feel that way?"

Evan smiled fondly and put his hand under the table to rest on Seth's knee. "A little, sometimes, but I bet you do too. I know you worry—and it's hard not to have anxious moments given what we do."

Seth looked away. "I just want you to be happy. I dragged you into this."

"You saved my life," Evan corrected. "And because of you, I have a home, friends, a purpose—and a very sexy boyfriend."

Evan hesitated. "And I signed up to go on an overnight orientation tomorrow at Summit."

Seth's eyes widened. "You what?"

"It's our best chance to get a look at the lodge and size the place up without attracting attention." Evan knew how much Seth was going to hate the idea. "Plus, there's this weird symbol on all their materials, and I think it might be the anchor, and the spa has a pool in a cave, like in Drake's vision." He pulled out the brochure and showed Seth. "It's got to be at the lodge."

"You want to go there overnight—alone? Evan, Swain's a witch disciple, and you're a descendant. You're taking an awful chance."

"I know. And I won't be able to wear a wire up there or use my cell phone."

"Evan—"

"If we go together, it will tip our hand," Evan argued. "Travis has magic, so they'll pick up on him. Drake's local—that wouldn't fly."

"Then take Brent," Seth said. "There's no reason for him to be recognized; he doesn't have psychic abilities, and at least you'd have backup."

Evan could see how much Seth disliked the idea, but his compromise made sense and quelled the nervousness Evan felt about the ploy. "Okay. There's a phone number on here. I'll call Jennifer and get Brent registered. You break it to Brent that he's my plus-one."

Minutes later, it was settled. Seth didn't voice his worry, but they showed clearly in his eyes.

"Thank you for trusting me." Evan gave Seth's hand a squeeze beneath the table. "And for believing that I can handle myself."

"I still don't like it," Seth grumbled. "But you're right about us needing to get a look at the lodge, and if you locate the anchor, that's going to be a big win. Just please…be careful."

Evan met his gaze and put his whole heart into his eyes. "I promise."

Lacey's seemed busier than usual, and as Evan watched Cameron behind the bar, he realized that there should have been a second bartender given the size of the crowd.

Evan excused himself and headed over to talk to Cameron. "Did someone call off? You look swamped."

Cameron wiped the back of his hand across his face. "Yeah, we're supposed to have someone who can float between the bar and the kitchen depending on where he's needed most, and I don't know where he is, but he's not here."

"I'm no good in the kitchen, but I've logged a lot of hours behind a bar," Evan said. "Happy to lend a hand if it would help."

"You're on," Cameron told him. Evan grabbed an apron and tied it around his waist. After a quick recap of the oddities of this particular bar's setup, Evan dove in and started mixing drinks.

He looked up and saw Seth watching him with a look that seemed proud and pensive all at once.

I'm going to need to drive the point home that I don't want to be doing anything else for now or be anywhere else. Evan figured that Seth was concerned he had derailed Evan's ambitions.

Before I met Seth, I was lonely, disillusioned, and had a target on my back, although I didn't know it yet. Despite the danger, I met the love of my life, and I'm satisfied with our lives. There's purpose galore, and I have my design work too. I'm happy right where I am—and I need to get that through Seth's thick skull.

Although it had been a while since Evan last tended bar, he fell back into the groove almost immediately. Chatting with the customers gave him an opportunity to size up any potential threat, and he could keep an eye on the door and the people playing the machines without being obvious.

"You're new," one of the men at the bar said.

"Just helping out," Evan replied. "Cameron's the real star."

"He's a good kid," the man said. He had a shock of white hair combed over a mostly bald head and a lined face that suggested a life-time working outdoors. "Don't know why he sticks around this town. Especially with the family curse and all."

Evan stole a look toward Cameron, but he was busy at the other end of the bar. "Curse?" He was curious to see what the locals made of the deaths in Cameron's family.

The man thumped his empty beer bottle down on the bar and nodded for Evan to bring him another. "Nice folks, it's a shame how things happened."

"I'm not from around here." Evan hoped that would prompt an explanation. He knew Cameron's side and had insight into the truth about the witch disciple's part in the tragedies, but he wondered how it looked to outsiders.

"The family's been here for quite a while, hundred years or so, I'd guess. But from what I hear, bad luck followed them. His dad died in a truck accident. Someone else drowned up at the lake on the mountain—never found the body, so I hear tell. And then more than one fellow just disappeared. Probably ran off with a pretty girl but didn't leave a note or anything," the barfly continued.

"Don't get me wrong—he's a mighty fine bartender, and I'd hate to lose him, but I gotta wonder if it might be good for him to get a fresh start somewhere else, know what I mean?"

Evan did, and while it wasn't his place to say that Cameron had plans to move on, he could understand even more why he and Tyler needed to get out of Buckhannon.

"Sometimes you gotta leave home to get a fresh perspective." Evan amiably agreed with the man, although he knew that for Cameron, the reasons went much deeper.

The next few hours passed in a blur as Evan moved with the ease of long practice, stepping around Cameron like they had choreographed the routine. Things finally slowed after supper, and Evan joined Cameron for a moment of peace in the kitchen.

"Thanks. You're a lifesaver," Cameron said, still a little flushed from the busy evening.

"It's nice to know I haven't lost my touch," Evan replied. "You're a real favorite with the regulars."

Cameron chuckled. "The previous bartender was a grumpy cuss who had a salty opinion on everything, so I've heard. Jeff, the guy who fills in for me and works on my day off, is good at mixing drinks but doesn't really get into the people side of things. It's a tough balance, and if you don't enjoy the social side, you can get worn down quick."

Evan usually enjoyed the chitchat, but he remembered days when he would have rather been left alone and still needed to give the customers a good experience. That could be exhausting, although not nearly as much as chasing down a wendigo or restless spirits. *I have a very strange standard for comparison.*

"Hey, can I ask you something?" Cameron glanced toward the bar to make sure no one was beckoning for service.

"Sure. What's on your mind?"

"You and Seth are *together*, right?"

Evan nodded, surprised that Cameron even needed to ask. "Yeah. For a little over a year now. Given the circumstances, it's been a bit of a trial by fire."

Cameron looked nervous. "You and Seth are the only other couple like us I've ever met."

"You mean gay?"

"Yeah. We're both from around here, and most of the locals just pretend they don't notice. We're careful in public. Tyler played football in high school and went into the Army, and everyone just sorta gave me a pass because I was friends with the right people. But West Virginia isn't the easiest or safest place to be out."

"Neither is Oklahoma, where I used to live. I understand."

"So I just wanted to say that seeing you two together, it kinda gives me hope that Tyler and I can make it."

Evan doubted Cameron had many people he could be so candid with, and his heart ached for him. "We travel around to do what we do. In some places people don't care at all, and other times we have to be more careful. There's usually someone trying to kill us for completely different reasons. But I wouldn't trade our life for anything because we're together. And someday, when this is all over, we're going to walk away and make a different life for ourselves."

"Try to avoid the getting killed part." Cameron laughed nervously. He saw movement at the bar. "Guess we need to get back to work."

Half an hour before Lacey's closed, Tyler came into the bar and took a spot at the end of the counter. Cameron brought him a Coke without needing to be asked. Tyler looked tired. Evan noticed that he had a gun in a holster under his jacket.

"Take your time," Tyler told Cameron as he accepted the soda gratefully. "I'm here to drive you home."

"See anyone loitering in the lot?" Evan moved past Cameron to fix a drink.

"No—but you can be sure I'll check again before it's time to go," Tyler replied.

"Take Seth with you. Safety in numbers." After the Renou-Vous presentation earlier in the day, Evan couldn't shake the feeling that Swain was just biding his time to make the next move—soon.

The bar closed without incident. Seth and Evan drove behind Cameron and Tyler and repeated their check of the area around the house and a sweep of the interior.

"Looks good," Seth told them. "Stay inside, and call us if anything weird happens, or if you even have a bad feeling. Trust your gut."

On the way back to the RV, a call came through, and Seth hit accept. "Hey, Brent."

"Is it too late to get together?" Brent's voice filled the cab. "Drake's back from the Hub, and Travis had some thoughts about the event at the library."

"We'll be there," Seth promised after confirming with a glance to Evan.

Evan wanted to go home and collapse, but he had the growing feeling that time was running out.

They pulled into the motel lot and parked next to Drake's car. Brent must have seen their headlights, because he met them at the door. Evan noticed the gun tucked into Brent's waistband.

"Sounds like it was a busy day for everyone," Brent said, waving them toward the twelve-pack of soda and six-packs of beer sitting on the kitchenette counter. Evan grabbed a beer while Seth stuck with a Coke, and they greeted Drake and Travis.

"I think we've got stories to trade." Travis waved them to find a seat. The table was littered with half-empty snack bags and pages of handwritten notes.

"Why don't Evan and I go first? Then Drake can fill us in on the Hub, and Brent and Seth can share what their research has turned up," Travis suggested.

Evan retold the tale he had laid out for Seth, sharing the brochure and map he had taken from the display and saved with a photo on his phone.

"I'm positive that the 'deflect magic' and auras charms helped me keep my wits about me," Evan said. "Everyone else seemed to be in a light trance. Not asleep, but not really alert."

"Do you know who the main speaker was?" Drake pressed.

Evan shook his head. "Peter Wellington, one of their guest faculty. I couldn't find much about him online other than his ties to Renou-Vous. I thought that his comments were generic and not exciting. Even so, plenty of people signed up for the one-night orientation, including me —and Brent."

"Like a timeshare," Brent muttered, and Travis rolled his eyes.

"Actually, that's what the presentation reminded me of, without the free ice cream or cocktails," Evan said. "Overly pleasant but very persistent and manipulative salespeople who practically lock onto your ankle as you try to walk away."

"Thanks for having my back and signing up," Evan told Brent. "Sorry to spring it on you."

"Pretty sure your boyfriend would have my head if I didn't," Brent grumped good-naturedly. "It's dangerous and reckless—but it's also our best bet to get a look at the layout and maybe find the anchor."

"The more I think about it, the more I'm sure that the 'family crest' is the anchor—if we can find the original version," Evan said. "Hiding in plain sight."

"I think you're right about the charm keeping you clear-headed," Travis replied. "I came into the library about five minutes after the presentation started so I could keep an eye on the doors. I definitely picked up a low-level spell to prevent interruptions—which would include letting people go in or come out."

Travis grinned. "So I sent a ghost. I gambled that the presenters weren't expecting anyone with abilities to show up, magic or otherwise. Mostly, I wanted to keep eyes on Evan, but the ghost reported that the room had a strange 'energy'—which I'm guessing was that spell. It might have made the attendees compliant, but it creeped out a ghost."

"The pitch was surprisingly non-specific," Evan continued. "But other than the orientation, the packages weren't cheap. I got the feeling that they didn't want a large number of resort guests, maybe just enough to provide cover for what they do up there, but not so many that they can't keep them in line."

"That actually makes sense—from a certain viewpoint," Brent mused. "Too few guests, and people will start wondering what's going on. It won't seem like a real destination. But Swain can't afford to have more people wandering around than they can keep track of. They might stumble onto something, and covering extra 'disappearances' gets complicated."

"He's also been canny about who he attacks," Seth added. "If someone vanishes and is never seen again every time there's a retreat, the families will force even the most corrupt cops to investigate, or go over their heads. So I think the events are a recruiting session of sorts. They accept the people they've already screened as potentially good sacrifices, and then observe them and get to know more details during the retreat. Later, they'll snatch them when Swain needs a boost."

"Not making me feel any better about this," Seth growled.

"Oh—and Drake? The spa at the lodge has a pool inside a cave," Evan said.

Drake's eyes widened. "Okay. Obviously that's something for you and Brent to check out when you get there. My visions don't always make sense at first, but there's a reason behind them."

A car with a loud muffler zoomed by on the highway, interrupting the conversation. Evan didn't miss how they all flinched at the sudden roar.

"About the whole 'corrupt cops' thing—bad news," Brent said when the car was gone. "We uncovered blackmail files on the cops, local and state politicians, and senior agents in the FBI and FBSI." He glanced toward Drake. "Bottom line—they're not going to lift a finger against Swain as long as those records exist."

"Not a surprise, given how I kept getting turned down and slapped on the wrist every time I brought up the missing people." Drake sounded bitter. He didn't ask how the "files" had turned up, and no one volunteered the information.

"I got into the Hub more easily than I should have been able to," Drake told them. "I dressed like the guys in IT, palmed a badge off someone I bumped into in the parking lot, and got by the guards, who weren't paying a lot of attention."

He reached for a beer, popped the cap, and took a pull before continuing. "Inside, there were bullpens full of data entry and call center workers. My suspicion is that they're not involved—just doing their jobs. The servers are on the two bottom levels. That's where the real action happens. Those were guarded, and I didn't get inside, but I didn't need to. I know where the rooms are, how big the area is, and I've got a good idea of where the emergency systems are. I can figure out the weak points. Freeze the servers, and we take down the whole operation. We were able to confirm that several of the other coven members are running their business data through the Hub." Brent appeared to be careful with his wording. "Money laundering, paranormal pharmaceuticals, and shifter trafficking—among other things. If it were any normal setup, we could go for RICO charges, but that's not going to work against a witch, and certainly not one who owns most of the officials in the state."

"I'm not surprised. And trying to escalate to get to authorities who aren't compromised would give Swain time to shut everything down and move somewhere else," Drake agreed. "The question is—how does the Hub fit into the bigger picture, and when do you want to make the move?"

"Swain's the big fish," Evan said and grabbed a soda. "We need to make sure he can't hurt anyone ever again. Knocking out the Hub will help in the long run, but we can't forget that Cameron's already been targeted—and he's next on Swain's list."

Travis turned to Seth. "You and Evan are calling the shots—it's your operation. How do you want to play it?"

Seth looked to Evan, who nodded. "Once Evan scopes out Summit, we need to get into the resort, destroy Swain's anchor, and find his ritual space. There are enough of us; maybe we can make the move on Swain and the Hub at the same time. But the clock's ticking, and I'd rather not be doing this after Swain snatches Cameron."

BASED ON EVAN'S MAP AND THE INFORMATION SETH AND PARKER HAD found online, they spent the next couple of hours planning how to infiltrate the lodge and destroy Swain's ritual chamber.

"I was thinking the chamber was likely to be somewhere outside the resort compound until the person at the event today mentioned the spa," Evan told them.

"Spa? Seems like a strange place for a ritual murder," Drake echoed, clearly skeptical.

Evan held up a hand. "Hear me out. One of the things the original Mountain Laurel Lodge was famous for was its underground spa pool —a natural cave with a mineral spring where people could 'take the waters.' If it's a real cave, there are probably sealed off areas that might be perfect for Swain's rituals."

Seth nodded. "I think you're onto something. So far, the witch disciples have preferred tunnels and caves for their rituals—probably because those places have energy that resonates with their magic. If there are parts of the cave that have been partitioned off since the resort was built, not many people would know about them. No one would have cause to go there."

"And he doesn't have to lure people into the mountains," Evan added.

"How does he get victims into the cave without attracting atten-tion?" Brent leaned over to peer at the map.

"The resort is inside the Quiet Zone, and that area has been less intensely mapped than other places," Evan replied. "But satellite maps exist—if you know where to look. Overlaying the satellite map and the map from the event, it looks like there's a supply road that comes up to the back of the building that is over top of the spa cave entrance. There might even be another entrance to the cave that's hidden. So my money is on the cave."

"Now we just have to figure out where he's hidden the anchor," Seth muttered. "The amulet that helps channel the ritual is something the witch disciples usually wear."

"Let me see the brochure." Travis reached out, and Evan handed over the paper.

"I've seen this before." Travis frowned as he pointed to an insignia. "The crossed keys behind a heraldic shield—there are usually a couple more elements, but it's a saint's symbol."

Brent took a picture with his phone and opened a website, then uploaded the photo to an image search. "It's part of the symbol for St. Louis Marie de Montfort," he told the others when he got the results.

"The patron saint of preachers," Travis added. "It's been simplified, but the essentials are there. Swain was originally a preacher before he joined Rhyfel Gremory's coven, right? And he's passed as a minister or evangelist all these years. 'Wellness mentor' isn't a big stretch. So it would make sense he'd appreciate St. Louis even though Swain wasn't Catholic."

"Maybe he's hiding the anchor in plain sight," Drake said.

Brent brought up the Renou-Vous website, which had a page dedicated to the lodge and a few photos of the interior. "Holy shit. They've used that symbol a lot."

"There." Travis looked over Brent's shoulder. "Can you make that bigger?"

The photo became grainy as Brent enlarged it, but even that didn't hide a glassed-in niche in the wall behind the main pool in the spa. Beneath a banner with the same symbol was an ornately carved wooden box.

"The location resembles where the monstrance is kept in a Catholic church," Travis said. "It's a fancy, deeply sacred vessel for holding the consecrated wafer for the Eucharist, and it's stored in an equally special elaborate box." He sighed. "There's so much hubris, blasphemy, and heresy wrapped up in Swain using that for his anchor—I'm at a loss for words."

"That's it," Evan breathed. "That's got to be his anchor."

"If so, then he's probably got protections around both the anchor and the entrance to the hidden cave," Brent pointed out. "So we'll need to have a plan to deal with those."

"Not to mention getting in and out," Seth said. "The spa is beneath the main lodge building. We might be able to get in and out through the back entrance if we just needed to access the cave—but somehow we've got to get to the anchor first in the main spa."

"Let's start there with research tomorrow." Travis stretched. "Seth should have more reports. We can double down on strategy, and we'll know more after Brent and Evan make their reconnaissance."

Evan had already texted Parker asking for additional maps and satellite images and figured his night owl brother would probably have results in his email the next morning.

"Tyler is guarding Cameron tomorrow," Seth said as they got up to leave. "So it's a good day for Travis and Drake and me to finalize plans and decide when to go after Swain and the Hub. Better get some rest while you can."

Evan suspected that plunging himself into strategizing would also keep Seth from going crazy with worry.

They thanked Brent, Travis, and Drake and headed back to the RV. Seth and Evan were silent on the ride back, not saying anything until they had parked and done their usual security check.

"You're quiet," Seth observed as they locked the door behind them and renewed the wardings.

"I could say the same."

"What are you thinking?" Seth hung up his coat and toed off his shoes as Evan shed his outerwear.

"We're close to nabbing Swain—that worries me," Evan admitted.

"Why?"

Evan loved that Seth didn't try to minimize or talk him out of his concerns. "Swain has to know we're here and that we're coming for him.

We've never seen one of the witch disciples back down yet because they all think they're too powerful to beat. So either he's biding his time for us to come to him—and then he thinks he'll destroy us—or he's got a plan to make a first strike. Either way, the shit is going to hit the fan soon."

"It's brave of you to infiltrate the Summit," Seth murmured. "I love that about you, even though I hate having you risk yourself."

"I don't like it either. Unless you've got another idea, it's the best option we've got."

"Believe me, I'll be trying hard to think of an alternative until you step on that shuttle bus," Seth told him. "But I'm glad Brent is going too. You'll need to come up with a cover story."

"I'll say that he's an old friend, and we're on a road trip. We stopped in town on our way to see the big observatory and happened upon the event fliers," Evan said, selling the lie.

Seth nodded. "That could work. Please don't get separated, and don't take any extra chances." Evan could hear the strain in his boyfriend's voice.

He opened his arms, and Evan walked into the embrace, resting his cheek against Seth's shoulder. "When you were a soldier, did you like the going-into-battle part?" Evan asked.

Seth tightened his hold and brushed his lips over Evan's hair. "Not exactly. It's a different environment. There was an adrenaline rush anticipating the action and danger, but underneath it, we were all scared. So being a bunch of teenagers, we tried to out-cool each other and pretend we weren't afraid. Being scared is normal, reasonable—and human."

"I know that—in my head. It doesn't help."

"It never does," Seth replied. "Because there's a real reason to be afraid."

"I don't want to lose what we have."

"You won't."

"Neither of us can promise that," Evan pointed out.

"No, but going after the disciples on their territory, on our timing, beats wondering when they'll come after us," Seth reminded him. "And when they're gone, we're free."

Evan hugged him tighter, breathing in his scent, and pressed a kiss to Seth's throat. "I'm beat. Let's go to bed."

They stripped and slid beneath the covers, still in their briefs. Evan rested his head on Seth's chest, and Seth wrapped his arms around him. They didn't take it further than slow kisses, reminding themselves and each other that they were together. Evan drifted off eventually, safe in Seth's nearness, but his dreams were filled with everything that might go wrong.

8

EVAN

Evan woke with Seth sleeping close, a sure sign that his partner was nervous. He rolled over and pushed Seth's hair back from his eyes, then pressed a soft kiss to his lips. Seth blinked awake and took a few seconds to orient himself.

"Bad dreams?" Seth asked quietly as if their bedroom was a private bubble into which the world outside could not intrude.

"Some," Evan admitted, stifling a yawn. "I kept seeing our plans in motion, only they all went wrong." He shifted closer and put a hand on Seth's hip, drawing him in.

"Pretty normal," Seth replied. "You don't get visions, so it's just your mind running through scenarios, trying them all on to fit. But it probably means they didn't let you get much rest."

"It wasn't all night," Evan objected. "I think I got some good sleep in between."

"We're not alone on this anymore," Seth told him. "We've got Travis and Brent for help, plus Drake and Tyler. And we've got our friends and Parker hacking and doing research. We know what we're up against."

The coven were formidable opponents, and the task had gotten tougher once the warlocks realized they were being hunted. Swain's minimal reaction so far worried Evan and made him think the witch was biding his time.

"Thank you for being patient. I'm trying to be brave."

Seth cupped Evan's cheek in his palm. "You *are* brave. I've seen you be positively fearless. There's no shame in being afraid of something that's dangerous. You never trained for battle."

"I could argue that tending bar on a rough Saturday night ought to qualify me for something," Evan joked.

"It does. You've got better people skills than I do, and you can read a room. You're great at talking to witnesses because they don't get a 'soldier' vibe from you. And you're still badass in a fight." Seth sealed his reassurance with a kiss.

Evan pushed their sleep pants down, letting their morning wood spring free. He and Seth pressed their cocks together in their joined hands, taking their time, bringing them both off slow and easy within seconds of each other.

"Feel better?" Seth asked as he used his T-shirt to clean them up.

Evan nodded, then licked his fingers clean as a naughty promise. While that wasn't the most intense orgasm of his life, he had learned that taking the edge off and getting an endorphin rush could be the best medicine when tension ran high. "Much. We'd probably better get going. Travis and Brent are expecting us."

Seth groaned but didn't disagree.

"Okay, but I want to pick up breakfast biscuit sandwiches and coffee at the drive-through," Seth stipulated.

Since they had lingered in bed, showers were quick. Evan had set up their coffee pot on a timer, so it was ready by the time they dressed, and they filled travel mugs. Seth double-checked that the files from hacking into the Hub had fully downloaded while Evan made sure he had Parker's latest uploads. They packed their laptops, grabbed the weapons bag, and headed out.

"Are those breakfast biscuits?" Brent greeted them with a grin when they got to the motel.

"Manners, Brent. Manners," Travis chided in a teasing tone.

"What? I'm happy to see them—and happier when they bring food," Brent returned.

"There's plenty for everyone," Seth assured them. "Donut shop coffee too, although I figured you already have a pot going."

"There's no such thing as too much coffee," Travis avowed, taking the cups from Evan.

They ate while the food was hot, deliberately not discussing the case. When they finished, Travis and Seth gathered the papers and cups while Evan and Brent set up their laptops.

"My brother Parker has a friend who's really into caving," Evan said. "He showed Parker how to access archives of old cave maps and geologic surveys and some new software that makes an educated guess about where caves are located based on topological maps. Here's what he came up with for the area around Summit."

Evan turned his laptop around so they could see. "There's an old map from before the original Mountain Laurel Lodge opened. Back then, the cave itself was the attraction. They even gave tours. Later, when the lodge and spa were built, they closed off public access to the rest of the caves."

The map indicated the part of the cave that became the spa and showed more chambers and tunnels beyond the big room.

"Here's another map, still from the original resort, that has a little more detail and a few more rooms." Evan changed the image. "I don't think Swain is going to go too far, just far enough that people in the spa won't be disturbed by the screaming."

"There is that," Travis remarked.

"Parker warned that the software map isn't human-verified, so it's an approximation, but it also shows a larger cave," Evan continued. "I imagine the truth is a mix of the three maps, leaving room for changes over time, or errors—but it's better than nothing, and it verifies the existence of the most likely place for Swain's ritual."

"Nice," Brent said. "Your brother does good work." He passed around a bag of cookies, and everyone helped themselves. "I'll let him know. He loves helping, and I'm glad he stays a nice, safe distance away from the dangerous stuff," Evan replied.

"Teag and I have been looking at how to partition the servers at the Hub so we can isolate the blackmail and coven information and not damage the files for legitimate companies." Seth showed his screen as Evan closed his computer.

"We don't want to destroy the data because turning it over to authorities could come in handy if we can find someone who isn't compromised," Seth went on. "And we don't want to interrupt the honest businesses' use. Plus, it would be better if we didn't cause any permanent damage, legality-wise."

"Which is why we're planning a denial-of-service attack that shuts down the servers, and then we launch a bot that sections off the coven's files. When the computers come back up, the hardware is fine and so is the non-witchy data. Swain's people are locked out of the bad stuff until we remove the malware," Seth continued.

"I'm glad you and Teag are the good guys because you'd be really scary otherwise," Brent said.

"There's still the issue of confronting Swain," Travis pointed out. "I can rally the ghosts, but I can't—or rather, won't—force them into a confrontation. The 'deflect magic' amulets won't withstand a head-on attack, and while the hex bags my witch friend made are good for defense and distraction, they aren't weapons of mass destruction."

"In the past we've caught the warlock we were hunting during the ritual when he was vulnerable," Seth said. "If we're lucky enough to avoid the ritual, we're going to have to come up with something else."

"He's immortal in that he doesn't age, but guns and explosives work just fine," Evan clarified.

Brent pinched the bridge of his nose. "All right, then. Full nuclear."

"He can't complete the ritual without his anchor. So if we destroy it and his sacrifice space, he won't be able to get future power-ups from Gremory's spirit. He might do a Dorian Gray if he's cut off from his power and have his true age catch up to him," Seth said.

Evan got up and walked over to grab a soda, pausing to stretch. Distant odd banging noises from the parking lot made him wonder if racoons had gotten into the dumpsters.

"I wish it were as easy as finding a secret magic painting," Evan said when he came back to his seat. "If we can't destroy Swain, he'll still have the blackmail materials and enough magic to cause us a heap of trouble with the authorities. And we don't know for certain that he couldn't create another anchor or find a different way to access Gremory."

"We'll figure it out once we see the lodge," Brent said. "And we will do everything humanly possible to get in and out without being noticed."

Seth sighed. "Yeah. Because that always works so well for us."

9

EVAN

Evan had put on a brave face for Seth, but the butterflies in his stomach had turned to lead by the time the shuttle bus arrived. He felt relieved to have Brent as backup, although he preferred to partner with Seth. He and Seth knew each other's moves and anticipated one another's reactions. Evan didn't doubt Brent's skill, but that lack of familiarity could cost them precious seconds in a pinch.

"Nice shuttle." Brent nudged Evan with his elbow to get him out of his thoughts.

"Summit is a classy place." Evan appreciated the gesture.

The transport looked new, a white van with the Summit logo on the side. All fifteen seats were filled, two of them by Jennifer and Josh, their "guides" from the luncheon.

Colorful posters showcased the lodge in the advertising above the windows on both sides of the shuttle, with pictures of the buildings, spa pool, and serene visitors in Yoga classes or a meditation circle. Calming music played over the speakers, and conversation remained quiet between seatmates.

Evan guessed he was the youngest person in the van. Most appeared to be closer to Brent's age—early thirties—while a few were older. All looked prosperous enough to afford Summit's fees.

Evan didn't realize how hard he gripped his deflection charm until his hand cramped and forced him to let go. Brent wore a similar amulet. Their bags held salt, iron, protective hex bags, and a sack with magic-dampening properties to hold the anchor if they were able to steal it. Evan's pockets held his chalk and plenty of his rune coins.

"I hope the food is as awesome as they promised." Brent kept up their cover and distracted Evan. "I think the road to personal enlightenment starts with good meals."

Evan chuckled. "I'll agree with that." Jennifer had warned them that the resort did not allow drugs or alcohol. He suspected that Swain was more likely to manipulate people emotionally and with magic rather than to try to roofie them.

His thoughts drifted to hoping nothing significant happened in their absence and worrying about Seth's safety. Under normal circumstances, visiting a retreat like Summit would be a fun break, a chance to breathe deep and take a day off.

Beautiful mountain vistas unfolded as the shuttle labored to climb the steep road to the compound. While Evan appreciated the view, he felt vulnerable knowing that his cell phone wouldn't work so deep within the Quiet Zone and that he had no easy way to signal Seth if they got into trouble. He could still take photos and intended to document what he saw for when they returned.

When the van rumbled beneath an archway that read "Welcome to Summit," Evan felt a frisson of energy that he knew must be magic. A glance at Brent confirmed that his partner had come to the same conclusion.

But what does the spell do? Does it deter nosy trespassers or make visitors more open to suggestions?

Despite the charms they wore and their familiarity with how magic worked, Evan harbored no illusions about being invulnerable. His rote spells were much less powerful than the witch disciples' magic, and while Brent occasionally saw visions, that gift was unpredictable. Their skills had proven valuable, but a head-on confrontation was unlikely to go in their favor.

Evan felt no compunction to fight fair.

He caught himself twisting the silver bracelet etched with protective runes that Seth had given him and knew that Brent carried similar amulets.

Maybe Swain won't try any funny business for the overnight guests. Sucker us in, and then whammy the ones who sign up to stay longer. Or maybe he'll just try to make sure everyone leaves ready to give glowing reviews about the lodge and the programs to keep the locals happy.

Come to think of it, Evan wondered how many of the people at the luncheon and on the bus were actually from Buckhannon. Cameron had said the fliers weren't new and that the library hosted meetings nearly every week.

Did wellness pilgrims in search of enlightenment come to the small town looking for an entrée to Summit? Buckhannon wasn't a big place, and the New Age-y vibes of the Renou-Vous programs didn't seem like they would be a hit with the mostly blue-collar residents. Pulling in health tourism was one way to bring fresh blood to the lodge—an unintentional pun that made Evan cringe.

Nabbing someone out of their small group would be foolhardy and easily noticed. But if Swain evaluated the guests on their suitability as potential sacrifices and further analyzed them on their visit, he could engineer their later disappearances at his leisure.

"We're here." Brent's comment pulled Evan out of his thoughts.

The passengers filed out of the van to reclaim their luggage. Evan and Brent carried all the special items in their backpacks since they suspected their duffels might be surreptitiously searched before being delivered to their room.

The newcomers stood next to a circular driveway at the foot of the steps into the main lodge. Evan noted the mid-century modern lines of the building. But a clever renovation had updated the lodge, and he remembered Jennifer's comment about being "kitschy-cool." *Smart marketing. Appeals to the nostalgia crowd as well as having a retro-chic vibe.*

Josh jogged up the steps and clapped his hands to get their attention. "Listen up, everyone! You can leave your bags by the bus. They'll be placed in your room while Jennifer and I show you around. Then we'll come back here for lunch and a mingle before the evening's agenda."

"Don't worry—I brought a micro-camera," Brent whispered, apparently sharing Evan's train of thought. "I'll get photos."

Summit's setting lived up to the name, atop a rise with a panoramic view of seemingly unbroken forest and the time-worn ridges of the ancient Allegheny Mountains. The breeze at this elevation was cooler than in town, and Evan pulled his jacket tighter.

"We'll end the tour inside the main building." Josh trotted down to lead them with Jennifer beside him. "That's where your rooms are located, as well as the dining room, main meeting rooms, and spa."

They walked on, and several two-story buildings came into view. "These are dormitories for larger programs," Jennifer told them. "And the lovely chalet in the middle is our library, which is open around the clock and full of resources."

The outdoor pool was closed for the season. Nearby was a large patio with firepits, grills, and outdoor furniture. A small amphitheater had seating for lectures and live music. Evan had to admit that if Summit wasn't owned by an immortal psychotic warlock, it would be a nice vacation destination.

"I feel like I've stepped into *Dirty Dancing*, only with Jack Nicholson instead of Patrick Swayze," Evan murmured.

Brent laughed. "I was thinking along the same lines."

"There are nature trails around the compound, but please use caution," Josh said. "We're in the middle of the woods, and that means wild animals. Please don't leave the lit areas after dark for your own safety."

They returned to the main lodge. The lobby had massive windows looking out onto the valley and a big stone fireplace surrounded by comfortable couches that gave it the feel of a ski resort.

"Lunch is ready." Josh led them to a dining room that was a study in streamlined elegance. Evan looked askance at the buffet, only to find that the varied offerings were surprisingly good, as well as the "mocktail" punch the servers brought to each place.

"So far, their recruiting efforts are on point," Brent noted. "It's hard to turn down good food."

"What brings you all here?" one of their tablemates asked, breaking the ice.

Evan and Brent shared their table with two husband and wife couples. The speaker was a man who looked to be in his early forties, with the trim, tanned appearance of a runner or an avid golfer. His wife's razor-cut hairstyle brought the term "power couple" to Evan's mind.

"We came from Roanoke," the woman in the other couple answered. "We heard about the fantastic programs here and just had to see for ourselves." She and her husband might have been in their late forties and looked more like small business owners than small-town socialites.

The speaker looked to Evan and Brent and quirked an eyebrow. *Let them draw whatever conclusions they want to.*

"We were on a road trip and stopped in town to see friends," Evan told their cover story. He and Brent hadn't clarified their relationship and didn't intend to. Letting people make assumptions made it easier to request a shared room since neither of them wanted to bunk with strangers or be alone in Swain's resort.

"The flier caught our attention, and we figured it would be fun to see what was going on," Brent added. Evan wondered how often Brent had gone undercover back in his FBI days. He seemed to have a knack for melting into his persona.

"I wonder if this is one of those Transcendental Meditation places," the woman from Roanoke said. "Maybe someone will play the sitar."

"That's completely different, Linda," her husband said without looking up from his meal. "This is more like those people you watch on TikTok."

"You never know," Linda spoke up. "Sitar music and drums go with everything."

"Is everyone having a good lunch?" Josh bounded to the front of the room with the energy of a game show host, and Evan wondered if he'd had been a school mascot in his teenage years. Happy murmurs answered his question, and Josh beamed at his audience.

"If you liked lunch, wait until you see what the chef has for dinner! Here at Summit, we believe that food and rest are two key factors to renewing yourself—and core principles of Renou-Vous," Josh went on.

"You'll find a copy of our plan for tonight and tomorrow in your rooms, but I'd like to point out the highlights. After lunch, we have a guided relaxation shavasana with meditative music," Josh told them. Evan recalled that they had been asked to wear clothes that didn't restrict movement but that were a step up from gym wear.

"Some people use it as a nap," he added, and the crowd chuckled, "but if you can 'float' instead of sleeping, you'll be even more refreshed. After that, some time to stretch and then a drum circle."

Linda elbowed her husband with a look of vindication.

"Before dinner, we'll hear from one of our mentors-in-residence, Paul Wellington, who spoke at the library event," Josh continued. "He'll give you a brief introduction to our approach to wellness here at Summit for those who might want to return. You'll have some free time after dinner—my favorite things to do include walking the meditative labyrinth, checking out the library, or exploring the garden when the twinkle lights are lit," he suggested.

"Then tonight there will be live music and spoken word presentation to induce deep relaxation and help you let go of tension," Josh said. "I'll tell you about tomorrow's activities at breakfast. Go enjoy your day!"

The program seemed so normal that Evan momentarily second-guessed himself. *Swain's behind this. People disappear. Whether Josh and Jennifer and the other workers realize it, they're helping a mass murderer harvest his victims.*

As they walked around the campus and the main lodge, Evan kept an eye out for the shield and keys logo. He saw it replicated in artwork or painted on the walls of buildings, but nothing that would serve the purpose of a witch disciple's anchor. While he suspected the real relic was in the spa, he didn't want to assume and miss something important.

"I wonder if we'll get a tour of the spa," Evan said to their tablemates. "It looked very nice in the brochure. I'm intrigued by the idea of it having a cave pool."

"Ooh, that's right," Linda said and waved Josh over. "Can we see the spa? If it's half as nice as the pictures, I'll sign up for a longer program on the spot."

Josh beamed. "If you'd like to do that during your after-dinner free time, I can arrange a tour. Let me set that up and let everyone know. The spa is one of the resort's selling points."

Linda thanked him and looked quite pleased with herself. "It never hurts to ask," she told the others.

Evan and Brent lagged behind when everyone else filed out for the shavasana session, and made a beeline for their room.

"We probably shouldn't vanish right off the bat, or someone will get suspicious," Evan said as he checked his gear. "But I wanted to know if anyone went through our stuff."

"Nothing's missing." Brent looked through his duffel. "But I've got the essentials in my small bag, and I'm not planning to leave it behind."

Both men wore backpacks that didn't attract attention but kept questionable items and weapons close.

Evan glanced around the room. Two queen-sized beds, a small couch, and a writing desk with a chair filled the space. A window provided a view of the mountains. The walls were painted a soothing light blue with white trim, providing a clean, fresh feel.

"No television." Brent moved around the room to check for recording devices and nodded an all-clear when his sensor didn't go off. Evan followed, putting down a line of salt and placing protective hex bags, which Travis's witch friend had assured him would also keep them from being overheard.

"Hey, Danny. Any ghosts nearby we should worry about?" Brent looked like he was speaking to thin air, but Evan knew he was talking to his brother's ghost. He was quiet for a moment, listening to a voice only he could hear.

"Danny said we're clear," Brent reported. "He sensed other ghosts in the complex, but he didn't think any of them were dangerous."

"I thought Travis was the medium." Evan knew about Brent's connection to the spirit, but their connection intrigued him since Evan also had a minor ability to summon or banish ghosts.

"He is. Travis can talk to all the ghosts. I only hear Danny. Twins, you know." Brent shrugged. Even after all these years, pain glinted in Brent's eyes from the loss.

Evan only knew the basics of Brent's story, but it was enough. He also knew that last year, Danny had helped Travis and Brent go up against another demonic infestation and had vanished. Brent feared that perhaps Danny was gone for good, but the ghost had just needed time to replenish his energy.

"I don't imagine we could get much of a TV signal here anyhow," Evan observed, referencing Brent's earlier comment. "Although DVDs would still work."

"I guess we're supposed to focus on relaxing," Brent said. "I'm glad I brought a book."

"Thanks to Linda, we'll get a tour of the spa so we know where to go when we try to steal the anchor," Evan said.

Brent smirked. "Nice move, getting her to bring it up. You sound pretty sure that's where we'll find the relic."

Evan shrugged. "I could be wrong, but it would make sense to be there. Everyone will think it's decorative, but it's also handy when Swain needs it for his other activities."

"I did have another vision—just a flash, but worth mentioning," Brent said. "I saw lights, sirens, and smoke. I don't know what it means or where it was—like I said, it was just a glimpse. But I wanted you to know."

"Thanks," Evan said. "It doesn't sound good, but at least it won't be a complete surprise."

"We'd better go do the shava-whatever. Don't want them figuring us for the problem kids too soon."

"Shavasana," Evan said as they left the room and hurried to catch up with the others. "Corpse pose. It's how a yoga class ends."

"Corpse pose? That's reassuring."

"Don't knock it 'til you tried it," Evan replied. "I went to some community programs when I lived in Richmond. I probably would have done more, except someone was trying to kill me."

"Don't ya hate when that happens?" Brent snarked.

"So we size up the spa and look for the anchor when we get the tour, then play along with all the activities until we have a chance to slip away," Evan said. "We'll have to wait until after guests can use the spa since we don't want interruptions. Then we slip inside, steal the relic, look for the secret door to the rest of the caves, and get out before we're seen."

"Easy, peasy."

"We'd probably be safest if we stole a car and left the lodge, but that's going to be tough to do," Evan mused. "We can't call Seth and have him pick us up."

Brent looked thoughtful. "I wonder...Danny might be able to let Travis know to come get us, and then confirm to me that they're coming."

"That could work. Do you think Danny can travel the distance?"

"He's done similar things before. It's worth a shot. At worst, we sit tight until dawn and then fake a medical emergency," Brent said.

"That should work." Evan did his best to sound confident, though he couldn't help feeling that nothing was ever that simple.

10

SETH

Seth's phone rang late in the afternoon. He frowned when he recognized Tyler's number. Before he could say anything, Tyler spoke.

"Something's wrong. Cam's not himself."

Seth could hear the barely suppressed panic in the other man's voice. He glanced at Travis, clueing him in that there was trouble. "Okay, start from the beginning. *How* are things wrong? I'm putting you on speaker."

"Cam was fine when we left the house this morning." Tyler pitched his voice low as if he was worried about being overheard. "He was okay when we got to Lacey's. I checked all the doors and safeguards the way you showed me, and everything looked right. So I settled in at a table while he and the crew got ready for the day.

"Then about an hour ago, a delivery came in. I offered to help, but Cam had both kitchen workers, so he said for me to sit tight. It didn't take long, but when Cam came back, I had a funny feeling. Like it *was* him, but it *wasn't*." Tyler sounded frightened, and Seth couldn't blame him.

"What seemed off?" Travis asked.

Tyler paused, and Seth guessed the other man was taking a couple of deep breaths to get himself under control. "I've known Cam nearly all my life, and we've been together for a while now. So it's little things that aren't quite right. His smile is close—but not quite. He moves differently. My Cam is a loveable klutz. This one seems more graceful. His mannerisms are just a hair wrong. I feel like I'm losing my mind."

"What about the other two kitchen workers? Can you talk to them and find out whether something odd happened with the delivery?" Seth suggested.

"I tried to go into the kitchen—came up with some excuse—and Cam blocked my way," Tyler said. "I couldn't do much without making a scene. It's very unusual for me to go into the back, so insisting would have seemed strange."

"Is he watching you?" Seth asked.

"I think so. He isn't making it obvious, but he's keeping an eye on me. I'm in the bathroom to call you, but I can't stay long," Tyler said.

"Sit tight," Seth said. "We'll come right over. It sounds like Cameron's either under a spell or Swain swapped out a shapeshifter for him."

"You're serious?" Tyler sounded unsettled.

Seth remembered Drake's vision and shuddered.

"We think Swain uses creatures who can look like other people in his blackmail schemes," Travis put in. "Like the one you told Seth and Evan about, that you saw at the lodge. If Cameron's been swapped, the creature who's taken his place is dangerous. Don't be alone with him, and try not to act suspicious."

"Right. But where the fuck is Cam?" Tyler demanded.

Seth and Travis exchanged a look. "We think we know, and we'll fill you in. But right now, keep your eyes open, and we'll be right there."

By the time he hung up, Travis had already grabbed his gear bag. "Come on, looks like our timeline just moved up."

"Evan and Brent have only been gone a few hours. And up in the Quiet Zone, there's no way to warn them or tell them about Cameron. I knew this was going to turn into a clusterfuck." Seth followed Travis outside.

"Having them go to Summit made sense," Travis reminded him. "We didn't expect Swain to make his move so fast."

"I know. But now it's even more complicated," Seth growled. "Just like always."

When they pulled into the parking lot at Lacey's, Seth drove his truck around to the back. Travis followed in the Crown Vic.

"Okay, Travis, go to the kitchen door. Get the workers out, ask if anything weird happened, and send them home. Pull the fire alarm," Seth directed.

"I'll go through the front and work with Tyler to get the patrons out. Whether it's a shifter or Cameron's under a spell, he's not going to go easily."

Seth jogged to the front of the bar and waited until he heard the fire alarm before opening the door.

"Everyone out!" Seth shouted. Cam seemed frozen as Seth took charge. Tyler urged the gamblers at the video machines to head outside, refusing to take no for an answer.

"Closed for the day for safety reasons," Tyler told the patrons. "Come back tomorrow." The customers grumbled but headed toward their cars.

Finally, they were all gone except for Cameron.

Travis came into the bar through the kitchen, cutting off his escape.

"What's going on, guys?" Cameron stayed behind the bar, tense and twitchy.

"What did you do with Cam?" Tyler demanded.

The creature wearing Cameron's face stared at Tyler as if he'd lost his mind. "What are you talking about? Did you hit your head?"

"You're not him."

Cameron's doppelganger spread his arms. "Ty, I'm right here."

Seth hadn't known Cameron long, but even he could tell that there was something not quite right about the way this version spoke and held himself. *Definitely a shifter.*

"He's not wearing the silver charm," Tyler pointed out. "It's not Cameron."

Cameron jumped the bar and broke for the door. Tyler tackled him, pulling him to the floor and wrestling to keep hold. Travis began chanting, calling the ghosts for backup, and the temperature in the bar plummeted.

Under normal circumstances, Seth figured Cameron and Tyler would be evenly matched, except for Tyler's combat training. This version of Cam was giving Tyler a thrashing.

Seth piled on and pulled Tyler and the doppelganger apart. Seth snapped a pair of silver handcuffs on the creature, who hissed as the metal reacted with his skin. He gave the man a thorough pat-down to make sure he had no weapons, phone, or tracking devices. Tyler snatched back the items he recognized as Cameron's and pocketed them.

Travis watched to make sure no patrons were returning while Seth and Tyler dragged the shifter out the back door and threw him in the trunk of Travis's Crown Vic.

Travis flipped the sign to "Closed" and followed them.

Seth was already on his phone. "Drake—we need a place to stash someone for a little while, out of the way. Somewhere unofficial. Can you help?"

Seth listened and then nodded. "Okay, thanks. Meet you there." He looked to the others. "He's got a cabin twenty minutes outside of town. Let's go."

Tyler looked spooked. "What are you going to do to the thing pretending to be Cam?"

"Nothing fatal," Seth assured him. "But we need to find out where Cameron is, confirm who sent the shifter, and keep him sidelined until this is over. There's no point in letting him run back to Swain and tell tales or have him show up so we fight him again. Just think about it as we're swapping one kidnapping for another."

Tyler swallowed hard. "Do you think Cam's okay?"

Seth didn't want to imagine how hard this was for Tyler, who had held up well when it came to accepting the supernatural and the idea of the coven.

"Swain wants Cameron alive." Seth did his best to sound positive without giving false hope. "I think he's okay for now. We're going to do everything we can to get him back safe."

Tyler nodded, stoic although Seth suspected he was barely holding it together. "What is that thing?"

"A shapeshifter, but I don't know what kind yet," Travis replied.

"You mean a werewolf?"

Evan shook his head. "No. Werewolves only turn into wolves. A shapeshifter like the one you saw at the lodge can appear to be anything—another person, a dog, a deer. They're born with the ability, not turned or bitten."

"How common are they?" Tyler sounded aghast.

"Hard to know because unless you test them with silver, you can't be certain who is and who isn't," Travis said. "Most of them don't bother anyone, so we don't bother them. Being a supernatural creature isn't a crime. Using those abilities to break the law and hurt people is."

"I just want to save Cam," Tyler said.

"So do we. And we're going to do our damnedest," Seth vowed.

Drake's cabin nestled in a secluded area down a dirt road. He sat on the bumper of his truck, waiting, when they pulled up.

"Is this out of the way enough?" Drake raised an eyebrow.

"Should be perfect," Seth replied.

"I'm probably required to remind you that kidnapping is a federal offense." Drake's tone made it clear his words were a formality.

"If it's a creature who isn't human and therefore doesn't legally exist, and he's already kidnapped someone else, I don't think it counts," Travis answered.

The doppelganger banged on the trunk lid from the inside, and his muffled curses were clear in intent even if the words didn't quite carry.

"Shut the fuck up," Seth said and thumped the trunk with his fist.

"Hey—don't dent the car!" Travis protested.

"Can you?" Seth asked Travis, who seemed to understand without needing the rest of the sentence.

Travis closed his eyes, and his lips moved silently as he called to nearby ghosts. The temperature fell, and a second later, the shifter in the trunk gave a frightened yelp.

"No funny stuff when we get you out, or we'll feed you to the ghost—got that?" Seth yelled. Silence amounted to agreement. Seth opened the trunk while Travis looked on with an expression of concentration that told Seth the medium was communicating with ghosts.

"Is that—" Drake asked, startled.

"Not Cameron," Seth hurried to tell him. "Shifter. We want some answers, and figured we needed somewhere more private. Thanks for helping us."

Drake sighed. "In for a penny, in for a pound. The cabin has basic wardings, but you can add anything you need to keep him contained."

"Don't worry—we're not going to kill him unless he attacks us." Tyler gave the cuffed shifter a shake. "But that doesn't rule out making him real uncomfortable until he talks."

"I've called to the local spirits, and they have agreed to guard the cabin," Travis said. "Crossing their line would be extremely uncomfortable, and they could haunt him," he added, looking at the defiant man.

Tyler hustled the shifter into the cabin, and the others followed. Seth figured the chill in the air was from Travis's ghostly friends, but he was glad for their help. Inside, Drake locked the door, and Tyler pushed their prisoner to the floor. The silver cuffs left red, angry marks on his skin.

"We know you're a shifter," Seth told the man who still looked like Cameron.

"You're crazy."

"Silver doesn't react to humans," Seth said. "So you can drop the charade. Where's the real Cameron?"

"I don't know what—" The imposter's protest cut off as Seth laid the flat of a silver knife against his neck. A red welt rose immediately.

Tyler stepped back, looking sick.

I can understand, Seth thought. *He knows it's not Cameron, but it looks like him, and we're roughing up the thing that's wearing his boyfriend's face.* Seth turned his attention back to the shifter.

"Look, we can do this all day, which is no fun for you or us. So make it easy on yourself. Where's Cameron?"

"Go fuck yourselves." The voice was right, but the way Cameron's expression twisted in hatred was all wrong.

"Maybe later," Seth replied in a dry tone. "This can get very unpleasant very fast. It doesn't have to. Ever bathed in a tub of water laced with colloidal silver? 'Exfoliation' doesn't quite cover it."

The creature couldn't hide a shudder.

Drake's eyes went wide, but he stayed quiet.

"Who sent you?" Seth advanced with the silver knife, and the shifter shrank back.

"Whoever sent you isn't going to rescue you," Travis pointed out. "You're expendable to them. In fact, they might want to get rid of you anyway so there aren't any witnesses. Think about that before you protect them."

"A guy told me he wanted to grab the bartender and not have anyone notice for a while, and the pay was good," the shifter said.

"Does everyone in town know you're a shifter?" Tyler challenged. "You're going to have to do better than that." Seth took a half step forward with the knife.

"My boss at the Hub—okay?" the prisoner blurted, eying the knife. "His name is Curt. I do jobs for him when he needs a stand-in."

"You mean when he wants you to impersonate someone?" Seth pressed. "Like on videos?"

"Yeah, all right. Sometimes. Or for conversations. Nothing major," the shifter answered, still surly. "No big deal."

"Oh, it definitely is a big deal," Drake assured him. "But if you cooperate, maybe you can plead down. We can protect you."

"The fuck you can. He's a goddamned witch!"

"Who?" Drake pushed back.

"Swain. The guy in charge of everything," the shifter snapped.

"Where did they take Cameron?" Seth didn't let up.

"I heard them say they were taking him to the Hub," the prisoner replied. "That's all I know. I was just supposed to keep anyone from noticing he was gone for as long as possible and then get away."

Seth knew from the look on Travis's face that he didn't believe the shifter or at least doubted the information.

"Here's how this is going to go down," Seth told him. "We're going to fasten your cuffs to something that won't move. You'll be gagged. We won't leave you long without food, water, or a bathroom break, but we can't risk letting you go."

"We're a long way from anywhere, so even if you could make noise, no one's around to hear it," Travis added. "The silver should stop you from shifting, but just in case, my ghost friends are going to make sure you don't leave the cabin."

The shifter didn't try to fight them as Seth snapped another pair of silver cuffs around his bare ankles and ran a chain Drake supplied through the cuffs to a support post for the loft. Tyler found a dish towel in the kitchen and used it as a gag.

"He's not going anywhere," Travis said. "The ghosts will make sure of that. Now we've got to figure out where they really took Cameron."

Drake locked the cabin, and they gathered by the cars. "What now?" Drake asked.

"There's no reason for Cameron to be at the Hub," Seth said. "It's too public, and there's too much risk of exposure. Swain is highly unlikely to do the sacrifice there for all those reasons. We know he stopped using the campground. So the most likely place is the resort."

"That makes sense," Travis agreed.

"If Swain wants us to go to the Hub—maybe we should," Seth said with a crafty smile. "Only not the way he expects. We go ahead with the DOS attack, set off the alarms, and clear out the place. Swain thinks we're going in after Cameron, but we do everything remotely, so we're nowhere in sight. His operation grinds to a halt, we cut him off from his illicit data, and while he sends his goons to intercept us at the Hub, there are fewer of them to come after us while we go into the resort."

"I think you're right," Tyler said. "And I'm coming with you."

Seth opened his mouth to argue, but stopped. He and Evan both knew what it was like when the other was captured or missing.

"All right, but you follow our lead," Seth warned.

"I was in the Army. I know how to go on a mission," Tyler snapped.

"Against normal people, yes," Seth replied. "How many century-old witches did you fight? How many times did you have to dodge spells or actual monsters? We're trained to deal with supernatural threats. So while what you know is valuable—it's what you don't know that can get you killed."

Tension rose as the two men faced off. Tyler looked like he might take a swing at Seth.

"You want Cameron back." Travis stepped in to break the impasse. "But Cameron wants you to be alive when he gets rescued. He'd never forgive himself—or us—if you got killed trying to save him."

Tyler's bravado waned. "Okay. I hear you. But I want to be in on the operation."

"Done," Seth replied, happy for the de-escalation. "We need to get moving. We don't know when Swain intends to do the ritual."

"I'll call Teag and let him know it's a go once we get back to the campground and have a signal," Seth said.

"What will it take for you to get your part set up?" Travis asked.

"Pushing a couple of buttons. I had it ready last night," Seth said, still being cagy around Drake. While the FBSI agent had proven helpful so far, if he turned on them they could be in big trouble.

"So we're all going to the lodge," Drake said. "If we need to tramp around in the woods looking for a cave entrance, we'd better bring good flashlights—and night vision equipment."

"I'll go back to the RV and start the program," Seth said. "I'll take Tyler with me; Travis and Drake can go on ahead in the Crown Vic. We'll meet up where Evan's map said the cave opened. If it doesn't— or if the cave isn't passable, we'll need time to find another entrance. Once we're at the resort, we don't leave without Cameron, Brent, and Evan."

"That's for fucking damn sure," Tyler said. "Now let's go rescue my man."

11

EVAN

Several hours earlier.

EVAN MANAGED NOT TO SLEEP THROUGH SHAVASANA—OR AT LEAST, NOT through all of it. Brent didn't snore, so perhaps no one noticed he was out cold. Evan had to admit that between the calm music and the restful pose, he did feel refreshed, and the stretches afterward worked out knots in tense muscles.

The guests filed into Summit's auditorium and took their seats, quietly buzzing about the day's activities. Evan was curious to see what Brent made of Paul Wellington since he hadn't gone to the lunch meeting. Evan wanted to get a second impression now that he knew more about Summit and Renou-Vous.

"People seem pleased with what they've seen," he remarked to Brent.

"It's had a vacation feel so far. What's not to like?"

"It reminds me a lot of church camp," Evan mused. "The first day was all fun and games. We didn't get into the guilt and hellfire until day two."

"Aren't you a ray of sunshine."

Evan shrugged. "I suspect the resemblance between the structure of the seminar and church camp is intentional. It's a proven way to manipulate people's emotions and get them to do what you want, whether it's signing up for heaven or a seminar."

Both Evan and Brent wore their deflection and auris amulets, and Evan wondered whether Wellington himself had magic or if Swain's power provided the nudges to sway the audience. So far, he hadn't seen pictures, paintings, or plaques mentioning Fletcher Swain, which was odd if he was the top mentor-in-residence.

Maybe he's keeping a low profile so it's harder to compare how he looks now to the recent past. It might not be time for him to "disappear" yet, but he probably has been around under this name long enough he should be aging—and isn't.

I wonder if that's why Swain's stepped up the murders lately. He might be "filling his tank" before a dry spell while he reinvents himself.

Making Summit less dependent on his presence made sense in a modern world, Evan thought. The lodge's programs and the revenue from the Hub brought in money without Swain needing to be hands-on, which would be helpful while he went into seclusion.

"And now we'd like to present our teacher extraordinaire, Paul Wellington!" Jennifer said. Recorded music swelled to quiet the crowd and focus all eyes on the stage.

Wellington bounded up onto the platform, looking tanned and vibrant. "How is everyone doing today?"

The attendees shouted back, a cacophony of positive words. Wellington beamed.

"You haven't even tasted what's for dinner yet—and I can promise you it will be a real treat," he teased.

"Now that you've had a chance to see the compound, meet some of our guides, and try some of the programs, I hope you're getting a better idea of how Summit and Renou-Vous can improve your life." Wellington slid seamlessly from cheerleader to salesman.

"In our introductory programs, we teach you how to relax. Isn't it funny that we need to learn that? We get so wound up with everyday living that we forget what it even feels like," Wellington went on, and the crowd nodded with sympathetic murmurs.

"Once you've made relaxation part of your life, it's time to move to the second stage in your journey—filling the places that were full of noise with something meaningful. Our intermediate-level programs let you explore the possibilities with the insight of our senior guides so you can find the path that's right for you."

The audience watched him in rapt attention.

Evan squirmed in his seat. Wellington came across as likable, a casual professor-type who might be pleasant to share a beer with at the pub. Yet nothing he said seemed particularly insightful, more like the bland generalizations popular with internet influencers. Considering the price tag of Summit's programs—and the risk of catching Swain's attention and vanishing—Evan struggled to see the appeal. Yet from the enraptured looks on the faces of the guests around him, Evan knew he and Brent were clearly in the minority.

A glance toward his seatmate confirmed that Brent seemed equally unaffected, maybe a little puzzled at the reactions of the others.

It's got to be some kind of spell. If it were something in the food, we'd be right there with everyone else. The only difference is that we have the amulets.

So we're going to have to fake enthusiasm, or someone will notice and get suspicious.

Wellington went on to describe the advanced programs and residency studies, but Evan tuned him out, studying the people nearby. Although Wellington lacked the fiery delivery of a tent revival preacher—and seemed bland for a motivational speaker—Evan recognized the expressions on the faces of the audience from his days in church.

They're hungry for something—attention, absolution, hope, a fresh start—and desperate to find someone to follow. Wellington and Summit provide that.

If people weren't disappearing and dying, I'd say it was none of our business. There are probably hundreds of programs like this, minus the homicidal warlock part. These folks can find what they're looking for elsewhere.

He knew those other seminars still carried the risk of narcissistic leaders who abused their power over the flock. But that danger, while significant, paled compared to bleeding someone dry on a stone altar to open a rip in time and space and summon an imprisoned immortal spirit.

Brent elbowed Evan, jostling him out of his thoughts as Wellington brought his presentation to a close.

"Welcome to the Summit family! We hope this is the first of many visits for you and the first step on a journey that will transform your life." Wellington looked pleased and humble as the audience clapped and rose to their feet.

Wellington exited the stage as the clapping continued. Josh stepped up to the microphone, letting the ovation die down. "Just think—that's not even a full lesson, just an overview," Josh told the happy crowd. "Imagine spending a full weekend, week, or longer, with time to dig into the program."

An appreciative murmur swept through the group. Evan almost expected people to wave their credit cards in the air.

Seeing how easy it was for a speaker to hold sway over a group made Evan shiver. Wellington himself might mean no harm—and perhaps did not realize Swain's darker purpose. Evan doubted that most of the guides or workers at Summit had any idea that the lodge was a killing ground.

But it was difficult not to take advantage of hero worship or blind trust. Evan knew that even those with honorable intentions often ended up falling prey to ego. As comforting as some people might find such a community—religious or secular—Evan was glad for his own found family.

"Next is dinner! Paul wasn't kidding about how good the food is!" Josh said, getting a round of applause. "Don't forget—you have time to explore afterward before the concert, so take advantage of a chance to have a look around and find your favorite spaces. Now head for the dining room and eat hearty!"

Evan and Brent hung back, letting the others file out of the room ahead of them. Knowing what they intended to do after the meal fueled the butterflies in Evan's stomach. He hoped tension and not a sixth sense of foreboding was to blame.

He wondered about Brent's impressions of the presentation,

although there were too many people around to discuss the matter right now.

Evan wasn't surprised when Linda and her husband, as well as their other two original tablemates, joined them.

"What did you think about today?" Evan asked after the server took their drink orders and offered a choice between "locally-farmed, sustainably sourced, organic, pesticide-free" chicken, fish, or vegetarian pasta.

"I'm coming back," Linda announced, although her husband didn't seem as enthused. Linda apparently didn't mind the possibility of attending solo. "It's exactly the sort of program I've been looking for."

"It's pretty up here, and the food is good," her husband agreed. "I've had to sit through worse for a decent meal."

Linda gave him the side-eye while Brent stifled a snicker.

The server came back with their drinks, bread, and salads. Despite his nervousness over their evening plans, Evan's stomach rumbled.

"How about you?" Evan asked the other couple, who still hadn't volunteered their names.

"I think I'd be even happier if it were just a resort without the New Age trappings," the man said, "but it's a nice change of pace. It wouldn't hurt to get out of the rat race and off the hamster wheel for a while." His wife nodded, more interested in her salad than in conversation.

"I haven't forgotten that Josh said he'd get us a tour of the spa," Linda told them as she tore into a piece of bread and slathered it with butter. "That's a make-or-break condition for me. I don't want to rough it while I'm pursuing enlightenment." She laughed.

"How about you two?" the other man asked. "Ready to sign on?"

Brent gave a pleasant smile. "Certainly thinking about it. They've given me a lot to mull over."

"The food is definitely a point in their favor," Evan agreed. "But I'm with Linda—I want to see the spa—and the library—before I make a decision."

True to his promise, Josh came to their table after their dessert of warm apple cobbler with vanilla ice cream. "I'll be outside the dining room to take you on the spa tour in ten minutes. We're just looking—not using any of the equipment or signing up for services this time—but you'll be able to get a good idea of what we offer. No one is ever disappointed!"

A few of the others had decided to join them, in addition to their tablemates. Josh led them down a wide staircase to a below-ground floor used for meeting rooms and then down one more level to the spa.

"You'll still have time to at least steal a peek at the labyrinth, library, and garden after we're done," Josh said. "I know I've mentioned them before, but they're my favorite spots when I get a few minutes to myself."

The lobby of the spa gave no indication that it was at least partially situated in a cave. Sleek wood, soft lights, and a small fountain set a soothing tone. They passed the reception desk and waiting area, done with a Danish-modern feel, along with a row of doors that likely led to massage or treatment rooms.

"The mineral pool is in the big space," Josh said. "It's a natural wonder and has been attracting visitors since the old Mountain Laurel Lodge first opened."

"Is the water cold?" Linda asked.

"It's...brisk," Josh replied. "But our guests come back time and again because they swear the pool has restorative properties. Spa visits are by appointment only. You'll find a full menu of services in your room. There's something for every taste."

He pulled on the door handle and looked surprised to find the room locked. "That can't be right," he muttered, frowning. "They're supposed to be open for several more hours."

Josh turned toward his guests. "Let me call their receptionist—I'm sure it's a mistake." He lifted the receiver on an old-fashioned landline phone on the wall next to the doorway and punched in the extension. Evan could hear the call ring, then a voice answered, but he couldn't make out the words.

"I'm very sorry," Josh said. "I've never had that happen before. The message said the spa closed early for a water leak and would reopen in the morning. I do apologize, and I'll see if I can set something up before you leave tomorrow."

He plastered on a smile, but Evan thought he detected a hint of worry. "On the plus side, more time for you to explore the other special places!"

Everyone was too polite to grumble, but Evan didn't miss the look Linda traded with her husband. The other man seemed put out, but his wife didn't seem to care one way or the other, and Evan wondered how someone so phlegmatic ended up at a resort to learn to chill out.

"I'll leave you here," Josh said when they were back in the main lobby. "Again, my apologies. I hope you have a great rest of your evening—the concert and drum circle are a real treat!"

"How disappointing," Linda remarked once Josh was gone. "I'd been looking forward to seeing what the spa has to offer."

"I'm sure we'll get a chance to see it tomorrow," her husband said. "Let's have a look at that library." He took her arm and steered her toward the outside door.

"If it's not too cold, a stroll in the garden might wake me up," the other man said. "Let's go check it out." He and his wife walked away, leaving Evan and Brent alone.

"I'd like to go back to the room for a bit." Evan knew Brent would catch his drift. They didn't talk in the elevator and remained quiet until they were inside, and Brent ran another scan for listening devices.

"What did you make of that?" Brent asked as Evan plopped down on the foot of his bed.

"Josh was definitely surprised. The spa wasn't supposed to be closed. I don't buy the 'water leak' story," Evan replied. "I wish we could call Travis and Seth to make sure everything's okay. I've got a bad feeling."

"Yeah, me too. Which makes it all the more important that we get in there tonight." Brent shouldered out of the small pack he had worn all day as Evan did the same, and they both took a moment to go through the contents, making sure they had the tools, defenses, and weapons they might need.

"We can't call them, but I can see if Danny can connect with Travis," Brent said, taking advantage of having a medium as a work partner.

Brent closed his eyes and took a deep breath. "Danny? If you can hear me, please find Travis and ask if there's trouble, then let me know."

He stayed quiet for several minutes. "Okay. Thanks for trying. Stick close—we might need to do this again."

Brent opened his eyes. "Something's up. Danny couldn't find Travis—that only happens if he's behind wardings or salt lines."

"So we're on our own, at least for now," Evan said. "And if Seth and Travis left the hotel room for somewhere more closely protected, odds are Swain's up to something. We might be the first responders if Swain's taken someone."

"I've got my lockpick," Brent said. "Now all we have to do is wait for everyone to be busy at the concert."

Evan couldn't shake the urgency he felt, but he knew that getting caught breaking into the spa would blow their cover and put their whole mission at risk.

"Once we get the door open, I'll go inside and steal the anchor—assuming it's there. You stay outside and guard the entrance," Evan said.

"What if Swain shows up?" Brent's expression made it clear that he didn't like Evan's plan.

"Then you can go for help," Evan explained. "I'll make sure there aren't any workers or stray maintenance people in the spa—just in case there really was a leak. But I've got a gut feeling that Swain wanted everyone out of the space because he has other plans for the cave behind it, and that can't be good."

Evan left it unspoken that he feared Swain had captured either Cameron or Seth—or both. *Or maybe he knows I'm here and figures one descendant is as good as another.*

"Shoot first and ask questions later." Brent relented, but still clearly disliked the choice. "I'll be through the door in a heartbeat to back you up."

"I'm hoping we won't run into Swain or get hauled away by the cops," Evan said. "And don't forget—if Swain's got shifters, the silver jewelry is our best protection and the only way we can tell the real version from the fake."

"Do you think there have been shifters among us the whole time we've been here?" Brent asked. "Is Wellington one of them?"

Evan shrugged. "Not necessarily. I guess it would be convenient to have a body double to fill in for you, but that would apply more to Swain than his lieutenants. And if the research we've done is right, the doppelgangers are for blackmail and fraud, so they're more likely to stick to the Hub."

"For all the times I thought it would be nice to be able to send a clone into the office when I wanted a day off, I think I've changed my mind," Brent said.

They waited in their room until the concert started. The small size of their group meant that their absence would be noted, but Evan figured they could beg off with a story about indigestion if anyone asked.

One desk clerk worked in the lobby. Evan and Brent watched out of sight until she went into the back office, then they slipped down the steps toward the lower levels. If anyone intercepted them, Evan figured he would lie about being confused about where the music event was being held, and they would try again in the middle of the night.

To his relief, they saw no one. As far as Evan could tell, Summit was largely empty except for their small group of initiates and the few staff members they had encountered. He didn't know whether there really were no other guests or if other seminar attendees were busy with lessons and meditation in another part of the compound. But he was grateful for having fewer people to dodge.

Brent took point, and Evan kept a lookout while his partner used a lockpick on the spa doors, to no avail.

"Let me try," Evan said after several unsuccessful attempts, changing places with Brent. Evan pulled some of the sigil disks from his pocket and chose the one he wanted, avoiding the need to draw a rune. Then he held the disk in his left hand while he placed the flat of his right over the lock and summoned the small spark of rote magic he had learned from Seth. He felt the energy tingle against his skin and warm the lock, which opened with a *snick*.

"Nice trick. You'll have to teach me that one," Brent said.

"Sure—after we get out of here." Evan eased the spa door open and peered inside.

"Whoa," he murmured, and Brent crowded in beside him to have a look.

The doors opened onto a large area that was a mix of natural cavern and human-fashioned cathedral. The ceiling and some of the walls were part of the bedrock, while arches and pillars made of stacked stone gave the huge grotto an otherworldly feel.

A waterfall flowed into a large, shallow pool. While the pool's sides and bottom were concrete, the deck areas were made from natural stone, and the water had a slightly emerald hue. Artful lighting illuminated the space while placing the focus on the cave elements, making the area seem intimate and fantastical. Comfortable loungers clustered in groups of two or four providing places for guests to read and relax.

"That's fancy," Brent sounded impressed.

"Look." Evan pointed to the wall at the back of the grotto. A glass case recessed into the stone held a painted, three-dimensional version of Swain's St. Louis Marie de Montfort crest.

"Watch the door," Evan said. "This is the best chance we're going to get."

"Be careful." Brent pulled the door shut behind him.

"You too," Evan murmured although Brent couldn't hear him.

Under other circumstances, the spa would be serene, tempting Evan to think about a couples' getaway. Now, Evan couldn't ignore a tingle down his spine that warned him to hurry.

He crossed the stone deck, skirting the pool, alert for any traps or odd sigils that might suggest magical protections. He didn't see any, and no guardians sprang from the shadows, making Evan wonder if Swain had relied on hiding in plain sight.

Evan reached the wall and stared up at the case. *It really does look like a relic in a cathedral. Swain's definitely got an ego.* He took a glass-breaking tool from his pack, the kind used for car wreck escapes, and pulled over a chair to stand on so he could reach the nook.

The case shattered on the first blow, and Evan froze, expecting alarms. When none sounded, he cleared away the remaining slivers and reached in to lift the relic from its place, feeling a bit like Indiana Jones.

He had expected the relic to be made of metal or ceramic. Instead, it was an intricately carved piece of painted wood that appeared to be ancient.

Evan's head snapped up at the sound of slow applause.

"Bravo. You've found it. Now whatever will you do with it?" Fletcher Swain stood in a recessed area of the wall, probably the hidden doorway to the cave beyond that Evan had intended to look for.

Swain looked unchanged from his old photographs—tall, blond, arrogantly handsome with a large, lanky frame. Evan would have guessed him to be in his late forties if he hadn't known the man had existed for more than a century.

Evan ran toward the doors. He heard a *click-thunk* as the locks turned, cutting him off from Brent.

"It was unwise of you to come here." Swain took a step forward as Evan moved away. "I knew of you and your partner—and your troublesome friends. You've gotten in the way of my plans more than once. No matter. You've done me a favor, giving me two extra descendants in addition to the Davis boy. A feast."

Shit. He's got Cameron.

Evan wasn't sure he would get out of here alive, but there was one thing he could do to help Seth destroy Swain.

He palmed another rune disk, knowing which spell it activated without needing to look by the feel of the carving on the back. Then Evan held the relic in both hands and called to his rote magic, speaking a word of power. Fire burned from his palms, engulfing the old dry wood, burning it to ash as Swain howled.

"Fuck you." Evan lifted his head defiantly.

"You're going to pay for that," Swain snarled. A gesture sent Evan flying, landing hard against the rough stone wall. His head spun, and he wondered how Swain would get his blood off the rocks before the customers returned.

Before he could collect his wits to protect himself, invisible hands swept Evan from where he had fallen and threw him into the pool. He landed on the water with a *smack*, and a force pushed him under, holding him below the surface.

Evan held his breath as long as he could, but Swain showed no sign of releasing him. When his burning lungs couldn't hold out any longer, Evan released his breath, watching the bubbles rise and knowing that he was going to drown.

I'm sorry, Seth. Evan stopped struggling, and he lost consciousness.

12

SETH

MEANWHILE…

TYLER PACED WHILE SETH AND TEAG COORDINATED THE DOS ATTACK, pulling in data Brent and Parker had found to pinpoint the servers so they knew which to include and which to leave alone.

"We don't have time for this," Tyler fretted.

Seth understood Tyler's jitters. "Everything's already set up. We just have to run the program."

"Why is it taking so long? We don't know what's happening to Cam or Evan."

Seth knew that Tyler didn't really want a lesson on the complexity of the hacking necessary to crash the coven's servers at the Hub. He had felt the same anger and impotence waiting to save Evan from dangerous situations. Seth knew that for someone with military training like Tyler, the urge to jump into the fray was even harder to deny.

Tyler looked at Seth. "You and Evan do this all the time. You put your lives on the line. Does it get any easier?"

Seth managed a sad smile. "You were a soldier. Did it ever get easier going into battle, knowing that not everyone would make it out?"

Tyler shook his head. "No. We just learned not to think about it, to push it down and cover it up. I was loyal to my unit. But I love Cameron. That's completely different. I can't imagine life without him. We have to get him back."

"Let's go." Seth ended his call with Teag and left his laptop running. He turned to Tyler. "We're going to find Cameron and get Evan and Brent back. Then we're going to kick Swain's ass.

"We have to leave our cell phones turned off and in the car," Seth told him. "That also means no walkie-talkies. Portable CB radios are permitted in the Quiet Zone, but they won't work underground, and they aren't secure. So once we're in, there's no way to let Evan and Brent know we're there."

TRAVIS AND DRAKE WERE ALREADY WAITING AT THE BACK ENTRANCE TO the spa cave. The unremarkable opening was partially hidden behind a stand of scrub bushes, easy to miss unless someone knew what to look for. The crack in a wall of rock provided a narrow doorway to a passage that led into the natural caverns.

Brent was with them, pacing and upset. Seth felt his heart sink.

"What happened?" He tried not to assume the worst.

"Evan and I broke into the spa to get the relic," Brent told him. "I was guarding the door. Swain must have already been inside and locked me out. I sent Danny's ghost to warn Travis, but he must have been somewhere Danny couldn't reach."

"The cabin." Travis looked from Seth to Drake. "Too much salt. Danny reached me once I left. We were too deep in the Quiet Zone for phones to work, so I couldn't let you know right away."

"Shit," Seth muttered. "Swain's got two descendants. It's the full moon. We've got to get in there and get them back."

"I went all the way through the passage to the door for the ritual room," Drake told them. "The path is clear, and there aren't any guards."

"The ghosts confirmed that there are three people inside the nearest cave room—I'm guessing that's Cameron, Evan, and Swain," Travis said. "The spirits saw an unconscious man brought inside through this tunnel earlier today—probably Cameron."

"Can they help out in a pinch when we go against Swain?" Seth asked.

Travis nodded. "I've explained what we're doing. They have witnessed past sacrifices. Some of them were victims. They aren't strong enough, even with my energy, to fight Swain for you, but they will do everything they can to help."

"Change of plans." Seth ruthlessly pushed down his worry. "Travis and I will go into the cave. We stand the best chance against Swain, and we've done this before. That lets Tyler, Brent, and Drake pull the alarms, get the civilians out of here, and avoid a catastrophe."

"Hell no," Tyler objected. "It's Cam in there. I need to help."

Seth laid a hand on his shoulder. "You don't have magic, and Swain does. If you get yourself killed, it doesn't help Cameron. But you can save lives. When the warlocks die, things get real bad, real fast. You're safer far away."

Tyler clenched his jaw hard enough Seth could see the muscle tic. "I won't desert Cam."

"You're not deserting him." Seth strained to keep his voice low. "We are wasting time. Please—we've fought the witch disciples before. We know what we're doing. Cameron won't forgive us if we get you killed."

Tyler turned away in a huff, and Seth let out a breath of relief.

"Good luck," Travis told the others as the groups parted.

"Same to you," Brent echoed. "See you on the other side."

Travis turned to Seth. "Take these." Travis opened his hand to reveal several silver bullets with sigils scratched into them.

Seth frowned. "What are they?"

"Runed bullets. The silver affects creatures, and the runes weaken magic," Travis replied. "Something new we've just started using—they work real well."

"Thanks." Seth reloaded his gun, keeping his original ammunition handy, although he hoped to avoid a shoot-out.

Seth led the way into the tunnel, with Travis behind him. They had heavy-duty flashlights, a duffel full of salt, weapons, and basic caving equipment. Each man carried a handgun. Seth checked before the group split to ensure they all wore protective charms.

While the damp rock smelled of mold and wet earth, the tunnel had clearly seen recent use. Fresh footprints were sharp in the mud on the floor. No roots or cobwebs covered the tunnel, and Seth could catch a faint whiff of cigarette smoke.

Movement stirred in the shadows. Both Seth and Travis raised their weapons.

"Don't shoot!" Evan stepped out of a depression in the wall, hands raised.

Seth froze. "Evan? How did you—"

A silver blade whirred past Seth's ear, slicing through the newcomer's bicep. Instead of a cry of pain or outrage, the creature wearing Evan's face howled as the cut immediately blistered.

"He's not Evan," Travis warned just as the shifter launched himself at Seth. The narrow confines of the corridor offered little room to maneuver. Seth grappled for the gun, still not sure he could fire on the doppelganger.

Up close, Seth saw that the shifter wasn't wearing any of Evan's silver charms. Its eyes flashed red, and the creature's supernatural strength was a dead giveaway. Getting shoved against the rock wall knocked the breath out of Seth, and he feared he was losing the fight for the weapon.

The shifter screamed in pain and arched back as Travis sank a knife into its lower back. Seth knew it wasn't really Evan, but watching Evan's face contort in agony still sent a visceral shock through him, and he fought the bone-deep instinct to protect.

"Help me cuff him," Travis ordered, leaving the silver knife embedded. "I didn't hit anything vital. Once the knife is out, he'll heal, but this way he won't come after us."

Seth tried not to look at the bloody shifter or the so-familiar face as he snapped cuffs on the shifter's wrists while Travis bound his ankles.

"Please, Seth, don't leave me like this," the shifter pleaded, copying Evan's voice and expressions perfectly. A deep-seated need to safeguard his partner surged through Seth, followed by a torrent of anger at the creature's manipulation.

"Fuck you for stealing his face," Seth snarled.

The shifter gave a pained smirk, teeth bloodied. "Almost got you."

Seth let his fury numb him as he shoved a gag in the creature's mouth. "Don't go anywhere."

"Can you pick up anything from the ghosts?" Seth murmured to Travis.

"Swain's setting up for a ritual. One man is on a stone table, and the other is tied up on the floor." Travis paused. "The ghosts say that the man on the floor made something catch on fire with his hands."

"The anchor," Seth guessed. "Evan must have gotten to it and used the rote fire spell. That's my boy."

"Another reason perhaps why Swain is intent on doing the ritual tonight, aside from the full moon. Without his anchor to store energy, he can't afford to let his power wane, and he can't draw on the anchor to bolster his mojo and help him open the rift," Travis replied.

Seth knew they were running out of time. The next turn brought them to the door between the cave tunnel and the ritual chamber.

"Ready?"

Travis nodded. "The ghosts are in place. Just say the word."

Seth set a small explosive charge in the lock. "Go!"

The lock blew open. Seth and Travis burst through the door, and Seth scattered a bundle of hex bags with disruptive magic onto the floor, spells designed to distract and cause chaos.

Smoke billowed, sparks flew and popped with a bang in midair. An impressive illusion of a dragon dove and gyred.

Cameron lay on a stone table, not moving. Swain, dressed in a ceremonial robe and holding a grimoire, stood beside the altar, chanting.

A circle of candles flickered around the altar, inside a space marked with runes and painted in blood. Evan lay in a puddle on the floor a few feet away, and from the position of his wrists and ankles, Seth could tell he was bound but appeared to be struggling to free himself.

Incense hung heavy in the air, mingling with the smoke from the candles and the hex bags. The temperature, warm when they entered, plummeted as dozens of ghosts streamed into the cave, shrieking. It was nearly impossible to tell the ghosts from the illusions, some of which appeared nearly solid.

Swain's chant stopped abruptly, and he swung to face them with a furious growl. He sent an arc of blue lightning, barely missing as Seth dove out of the way. Seth doubted his deflection amulet could protect him from a full strike, and he didn't want to test it.

Vengeful spirits advanced on Swain, no longer able to be hurt by his magic. Some were the barest shadow of their former selves, while those more recently dead manifested nearly solid.

Travis orchestrated the ghosts while Seth ducked Swain's blasts of magic to edge closer to where Evan lay.

"You have ruined everything!" Swain screamed and raised a hand to send another torrent of power toward Seth.

Free, Cameron jackknifed up and grabbed the amulet that hung around Swain's neck. He yanked it off and rolled to the floor, putting the altar between himself and the raging warlock.

Seth sent a streak of fire at Swain, forcing the witch disciple to hurl himself out of the way and distract him from Cameron. When Swain regained his footing, Seth clipped his shoulder with a runed bullet. The shot wouldn't kill, but it would hurt like a son of a bitch, and the sigils would drain his energy the longer the bullet remained in his body.

Evan had freed himself and crawled toward where Cameron hunched behind the altar. He laid out several wooden disks then drew another sigil with the chalk. Evan spoke the words of power, and the runes glowed, followed by a fiery stream to keep Swain at bay. Evan murmured another word, and the chalked symbol flared, then several stones rose from the ground and flew toward the witch, forcing him to lose focus swatting the rocks away or be hit.

Above the stone table, the air crackled and shimmered with a deep green glow. Swain swung back to stare into the anomaly.

"Master—you've heard my call," the warlock cried out as the glowing space grew larger and brighter, like a rip in a curtain that hid the sun. A man's shape took form, Rhyfel Gremory's tortured soul, trapped in a prison between life and death.

Evan and Cameron seized the moment to dodge from their hiding place.

Swain lunged, grabbing Cameron's arm, fingers digging into the flesh of his bicep like claws, and pulled him toward the glowing rift.

"Let go!" Evan held onto Cameron and jerked in the opposite direction. Seth added his weight, knowing that none of them dared be pulled into that deadly vortex.

"Now!" Travis's voice cut through the clamor.

The ghosts swarmed Swain, making him loosen his grip long enough for Evan and Cameron to jerk free.

Seth took a shot through the ghostly miasma and put a bullet in Swain's chest.

The cavern began to tremble with wild energies, showering them with pebbles and rock dust.

"Run!" Seth told Evan and Cameron.

Swain stumbled toward the portal, pulled by his dead master. He clutched at Seth, missed him, and tore the gun out of Seth's grip. Before he could turn it on Seth, Gremory dragged his disciple back into the maw of the vortex and vanished along with the rift. Seth nearly fell against the altar.

The portal's disappearance didn't slow the tremors, and larger rocks fell as fissures cracked the cave roof.

Ghosts shoved Seth back the way he had come. Part of the ceiling came down, blocking the entrance to the spa. Seth choked, and his eyes stung as the dust clouds filled the air.

"Come on!" Evan screamed from the back corridor where he and Cameron waited.

Travis dodged toward Seth, closing the last few feet between them. Travis half-dragged, half-carried Seth into the hallway. They took off running as the cave-in roared behind them, making the ground beneath their feet heave and buck.

"The shifter!" Seth said as they wound through the tunnel. "We have to get him out."

But when they reached the off-jog the creature no longer lay where they'd left him.

"He's gone." Travis took a step down the side corridor in pursuit, but Seth yanked him back.

"He's either managed to shift and run or dragged himself off. You can't find him, and we don't have time to look." Seth hauled Travis back to the main path.

Slipping, sliding, and falling, they plunged through the darkness on their way to the hillside entrance. Evan fell, and Seth pulled him to his feet, staggering toward the light.

They cleared the cave opening seconds before everything collapsed behind them with a deafening rumble. The shockwave threw Seth, Cameron, and Evan onto the ground, and they lay gasping.

"We did it." Travis coughed and choked on the cloud of dust that followed them out.

A horrendous roar made them all scramble farther away from the entrance. The hillside shuddered and crumbled as a huge sinkhole emerged that completely swallowed all traces of the lodge.

"Fuck!" Seth yelled as his heart pounded and his ears rang. He clung to Evan's hand with a vise grip.

"What about the people at the lodge?" Cameron croaked. "Tyler—oh, God. Tyler!"

Travis took a few seconds to get his breath. "They're okay. They got the civilians out. Danny told me."

Seth had never been so happy to have a ghost spy on their side. He turned to Evan and then Cameron. "Are you okay?"

Cameron rubbed the red marks on his wrists where he had been bound. "I'll probably have nightmares and PTSD for the rest of my life, but I'm not badly hurt."

Evan nodded. "I'll have some spectacular bruises, but nothing that won't heal. I could really use some dry clothes, though, since Swain tried to drown me. What about you?"

Seth remembered seeing shifter-Evan howl in pain and collapse with a knife in his back, a sight he knew he would never be able to scrub from his memories. With the shifter's body gone in the cave-in, along with Swain, Seth's gun, and the ritual chamber, no evidence remained.

"What about the ghosts?" Seth asked Travis. "They—and you—saved our asses."

"They're at peace," Travis replied in a quiet voice, staring into the distance. "They are avenged, even if the rest of the world never knows the whole story."

The four men trudged to their cars and inched down the mountain road, afraid the cave-in had spread or weakened the ground. Seth took the turn toward where the main resort building had been and held his breath, fearing what he would see.

Dozens of people milled at the foot of the driveway. Where the main lodge once stood at the top of the hill was now rubble and a gaping chasm.

"Travis!" Brent ran toward them when they got out of the vehicles. He clapped Travis on the shoulder, and they spoke with each other in quiet voices.

"Cam!" Tyler was steps behind Brent, searching for his boyfriend.

Drake looked up at their voices and grinned in relief from where he talked with the first responders who had just arrived on the scene.

Tyler swept Cameron into his arms, apparently no longer caring what strangers made of them. Cameron wrapped his arms around his boyfriend, clinging with all his strength. Evan took Seth's hand.

"It's done," Evan said, as the crowd paid them no attention. "Let's get out of here."

13

EVAN

"WE ARE DEFINITELY LEAVING TOWN," TYLER SAID. THEY HAD RETURNED to Drake's cabin to clean up and debrief, taking the evening to decompress.

"The sooner, the better," Cameron replied. They sat together on the end of the couch, still holding hands. "Thank you all for coming after me. You put yourselves in a lot of danger."

"It's kinda what we do." Evan glanced toward Seth, who was deep in conversation with Brent. Brent had already made a run to the motel to reclaim his laptop, just in case anyone traced them back to the attack on the Hub.

"What happened to the shifter from Lacey's?" Tyler asked. The creature who had posed as Cameron was gone.

"I let him go." They looked up to see Drake. "He had been forced to obey Swain. Now that Swain and his operation at the Hub are gone, he's free. I told him to stay out of trouble and not come back."

They took the opportunity to shower and change clothes, ridding themselves of the dust and dirt from the cave-in. Drake bustled in the kitchen, making a batch of spaghetti—quick, comforting, and filling. The smell of garlic and onions filled the small house, and now that they were done risking their lives, Evan's stomach rumbled.

Partial bottles of whiskey sat on the table after a hearty toast to everyone's survival and refills to soothe ragged nerves.

"We pulled all the fire alarms and set off the sprinklers," Tyler recounted. "Then Brent and Drake got people to move far away from the buildings. I think Drake might have flashed his badge."

"Brent's vision." Evan glanced at Brent, who nodded and then explained to the others.

Seth chuckled. "I imagine that would get people moving. Brent's ex-FBI, so he can certainly do the 'fed thing' believably."

Brent overheard Seth and flipped him the bird, although his grin softened the response.

"I understand," Tyler said. "It's like how people always know if you're ex-military. It just shows."

"Was everyone accounted for from the lodge?" Evan asked.

"As far as we could tell." Tyler seemed to be holding together well, but Evan knew that the real test would come after everyone else had gone home and he had a chance to process what had happened. "Josh and Jennifer were counting heads. I think there were fewer guests than usual, which was a good thing."

"If Swain intended to do his ritual on the full moon, having a smaller number of potential witnesses was smart," Evan observed. "It just didn't quite work out the way he planned."

They stayed the night in the cabin as if everyone wordlessly agreed that they weren't ready to part company just yet. Evan thought it was wise to lie low until they knew for certain that no one was looking for them, either from Swain's team or local law enforcement.

Nightmares woke Evan several hours after they had turned in for the night. He found Seth propped up next to him, intent on his e-reader.

"Couldn't sleep either, huh?" Evan asked, groggy.

"Nah, I didn't like what I saw every time I closed my eyes," Seth admitted.

He and Travis had told the others about the shifter in the tunnel, although Seth had tried to downplay the effect it had on him. That didn't fool Evan, who couldn't imagine anything worse if their roles had been reversed.

"You know that wasn't me in the tunnel," Evan said quietly, moving to put his head in Seth's lap.

"It looked like you, sounded like you," Seth replied, voice ragged. "I saw the reaction to silver, but I just couldn't shoot."

"I'm glad Travis was there," Evan said. In the darkness, their low voices took on a confessional tone. "Don't beat yourself up over it. I don't think I could have shot either if the situation was reversed."

"I was so afraid we'd be too late," Seth carded his hand through Evan's hair. "Or that we couldn't get into the ritual room, or that we wouldn't be strong enough to stop Swain."

"We did it—together," Evan reminded him, trying not to think about almost drowning. "All four of us and Travis's ghosts. Swain might have known how to fight off an attack by another witch, but we came at him with stuff he never expected. Ghosts. Fire. Runed bullets. Little stuff that added up."

Seth nodded. "I think the warlocks have gotten used to putting all their trust in their magic and dismissing everything else as too minor to count. So while we were technically outgunned, it actually worked in our favor because he didn't have a defense."

They were quiet for a while. Evan took comfort from the warmth of Seth's body and the gentle touch of his hand.

"I was scared," Evan said finally. "I was afraid you wouldn't know things had gone wrong until it was too late, or that you wouldn't be able to get to us. Or that you'd get hurt trying to protect me."

Evan had seen a hundred scenarios play out after waking, tied up in the ritual chamber, trying to get free. He hadn't known whether Brent had managed to send for help or if he had also been incapacitated.

Cameron's terror spurred Evan to come up with a plan, however unlikely, to delay the ritual even if he couldn't stop it. Evan had been resigned to die but intended to go down swinging despite the odds.

"Thank Danny's ghost," Seth said. "He saved the day by letting Travis know you and Brent were in trouble. The other ghosts made great spies, so we knew what to expect inside the ritual room. That helped a lot. And by the way—you and Cameron were badass."

Evan felt relieved that the cave-in had removed all evidence, requiring no awkward explanations about bullets fired from Seth's gun or Swain's missing body. Still, he was very ready to leave Buckhannon in the rearview mirror.

"Now that Cameron and Tyler know about the supernatural side of things, do you think they'll get involved with hunting?" Evan asked.

"I hope not. Someone deserves a normal life," Seth replied. He was silent for a few moments. "I know you worry that I won't be able to let this go once we've stopped the coven. That there will always be one more monster and one more after that. But I swear, when we're done, we'll be done for good. Someone else can take a turn. I want us both to live long enough to grow old together."

Evan pulled Seth's hand down and kissed his palm. "Me, too."

Sometimes, the adrenaline of the fight translated into hot sex. Tonight, the dangers still seemed too fresh, the things that could have gone wrong too close. Evan felt the relief of surviving without the exhilaration of victory.

Near-death experiences were real cockblockers.

"Before we take on the next witch disciple, we need time off," Seth said. "They already know we're gunning for them. A few extra days won't make a difference for the fight, but it will for us."

"I'm definitely in favor," Evan replied.

They stayed tangled up together until just after dawn. Seth dozed off, nearly dropping his e-reader. Evan shifted to avoid a crick in his neck, but they remained curled around each other for reassurance.

In the morning, they woke to the smell of coffee and bacon and the sound of Drake whistling in the kitchen.

"Gonna have to re-provision after this," Drake said as Evan and the others stumbled in, drowsy and rumpled. "You never know when you need a safe house."

"Have you thought about what you want to do next?" Brent asked as Drake put a platter of bacon onto the table.

"Quit the Bureau if I haven't been fired already," Drake replied with a sigh. "I figured it was better for me to deal with the authorities at the lodge than to let any of you get dragged into it. But I can't imagine my boss will be happy since this definitely wasn't one of my assignments."

"Thank you for that," Travis said. "You saved us a whole heap of trouble—and paperwork."

"It worked out to just let you all blend into the crowd," Drake replied. "Made for a lot fewer questions."

"If you end up looking for a new job, I can always use help—at least temporarily—with the private eye biz. Longer term, we have friends at the Tennessee Bureau of Supernatural Investigation," Brent said. "You'd need to relocate, but I'm guessing that wouldn't be a big deal. Let me know what you want to do."

"Much obliged," Drake answered. "I think I'll be taking you up on that once we get the formal firing process over and done."

After breakfast, they cleaned up the cabin, took inventory of supplies to be replenished, and finished off anything perishable. Then they drove back to town, gathering at the hotel where Travis and Brent still had a room.

"Thanks again—for everything," Seth said to Drake. "We owe you."

"Happy to help. Come visit after I move to Pittsburgh—or Tennessee," Drake joked, trading handshakes and back slaps before he drove away.

Tyler and Cameron still had a white-knuckled grip on each other's hands, which Evan totally understood.

"I don't know how to thank you for putting yourselves at risk for us and saving our lives," Cameron told them. "I'll let you know where we end up in Pittsburgh. And if we can ever help, just call."

Evan knew Cameron meant what he said, but he truly hoped that paranormal threats would leave the two young men alone after this.

"Good luck with the job search," Seth told them. "I'm just glad we were able to be in the right place at the right time."

Tyler had left his car at the motel while Cameron's was still at Lacey's, so they said goodbye with a round of hugs and headed out.

"Got a moment to talk about the Hub?" Brent motioned Seth and Evan inside.

Brent set his laptop up on the table. "You and Teag pulled off a real Hail Mary pass," he said to Seth. "I can search databases with the best of them, but I'm not a hacker. Take a look at what went down." He turned the screen so they could see the news coverage. "Hub Melts Down." "Data Center Blues." "Cyberattack Hits Hub Hard."

"Nice," Evan said. "Now please tell me that no one has a clue about how it happened."

Brent grinned. "Plenty of theories out there, none of them right. I stopped to have a look before I came back to the cabin last night. The 'experts' are debating whether it was a data breach, a coordinated attack by foreign powers, or a spiteful former employee. Oh—and since it just so happened to reveal the blackmail documents, local and state politics is on spin cycle for the foreseeable future."

"And the legitimate companies that used the Hub?" Seth asked.

"None of their data was lost or compromised. No employees were harmed—they didn't even realize anything was going on until it was too late."

"Teag and I got copies of all the coven records," Seth said. "I imagine we'll be parsing through those for a long time, but they might help us take down the rest of the warlocks."

"Of course, the Hub 'lost' all those records, so the other witch disciples are up shit creek with their money laundering and asset transfers shut down," Brent added. "They're going to be scrambling for a while to rebuild their empire. And with the Hub, the lodge, and the seminar program out of commission, Swain's business holdings are likely to be liquidated."

"How about the shifters and other creatures Swain was using?" Evan asked.

"Teag and I believe that most, if not all, of them were trafficked, kidnapped, and forced to do Swain's bidding," Seth said.

"Teag told me that he found a section in the basement of the Hub that was basically a prison with digital security," Seth added. "He turned off the locks when we attacked the servers. The creatures are long gone by now—and if they stay out of trouble, they're not our concern."

Evan saw the shadows in Seth's eyes and guessed he was thinking about the shifter in the tunnel. *I hate that he attacked Seth and impersonated me, but maybe Swain didn't give him a choice.* Part of him hoped that amid the chaos, the shifter had gotten away.

"I guess that wraps things up," Seth said as they walked to the parking lot. "Thank you both for dropping everything and coming down here. We really couldn't have done it without you."

Travis shrugged. "That's what friends are for. Let us know the next time you're coming through Pittsburgh. We'll find something distinctly non-dangerous to do."

Seth and Evan said their goodbyes and drove back to the campground. Evan held his breath, half expecting to find officers waiting to arrest them. He sighed in relief to find their RV just as they had left it.

"What do you say we blow this popsicle stand early and go somewhere else for a few days?" Seth said. "I don't even care if we get our deposit back."

"Somewhere out of West Virginia, please. Just in case," Evan replied.

The wardings were untouched, reassuring them no one had tampered with the trailer. Evan went to pay the office while Seth readied the RV to leave. It didn't take long before they were back on the highway.

They drove for more than three hours, heading south to Wytheville, Virginia, where Evan had gotten them another campground reservation. Other than discussing their destination's amenities, they didn't talk much. Evan struggled to reconcile everything that had happened at Summit and figured Seth was also wrestling with his emotions.

"The drive is beautiful," Evan remarked as they wove through the Blue Ridge Mountains.

"Probably why they call it a 'scenic byway,'" Seth snarked. "Thanks for the suggestion to go this way. The view is spectacular."

Evan reached over and took Seth's hand. "The view from here isn't so bad, either." He turned to look at Seth.

"Hold that thought until I'm not taking a fifth-wheeler down winding mountain roads," Seth warned but gave Evan's hand a squeeze, then put his hand back on the wheel.

The campground resort turned out to be even nicer than its website claimed, and while Evan doubted they would take advantage of all of the features, he looked forward to a few games of bowling and some time spent in the arcade.

Once they checked in and got the RV situated, Seth and Evan drove into town for dinner and groceries. Seth found a charming restaurant that was fancier than their usual diners and chains, and Evan gave him a questioning look.

"We saved the world again. I think that deserves a nice meal." Seth shrugged. "Can't I take my best boy out for a night on the town?"

"Better be your *only* boy." Evan was relieved at the normalcy of flirting after everything that had happened over the past few days.

"Always." Seth grinned.

To Evan's relief, the restaurant wasn't a stickler for dress code, despite the white tablecloths and upscale historic house setting. Its menu specialized in comfort food done right. Seth opted for a decadent Angus burger with Gouda cheese and sauteed onions, along with hand-cut fries and house-made pickles. Evan chose meatloaf in a sweet and spicy red chili sauce with homemade macaroni and cheese. For dessert, they split a slice of chess pie.

"I'd say that qualifies as a good celebration dinner," Evan said as they walked to the truck.

"Not done celebrating yet," Seth told him with a wink. "But we need to pick up groceries so we don't have to run out tomorrow."

They made short work of shopping, buying essentials for breakfasts and lunches as well as favorite snacks and a couple of bottles of prosecco. After putting the groceries away, they strolled to the chairs around the campground's large gas firepit.

"I love how many stars you can see from here." Evan snuggled close to Seth.

"Can you find the constellations?" Seth asked.

Evan shook his head. "No. I know my zodiac sign, but I couldn't find it in the sky."

"Jesse and I got on an astronomy kick when we were in middle school," Seth recalled. "Mom and Dad bought us a telescope for Christmas, and we camped in the backyard whenever the weather was decent, looking for meteor showers and asteroids and learning to find the stars."

He sounds wistful, as he always does when he remembers Jesse, Evan thought, and wished that Seth's happy memories of his brother weren't always tinged with sadness.

"You can teach me," Evan said. "I've always wanted to know that stuff. But no tent camping. I only glamp."

Seth chuckled. "I think the RV counts as 'glamping.' But if you'd like, we can string twinkle lights and sheer curtain swags for the right ambiance."

"Well, we'd certainly be the talk of the trailer park," Evan said. "But I'm fine the way we are."

The wind picked up, and despite the fire, Evan rubbed his hands together for warmth.

"I have a better idea of how to warm up," Seth murmured next to his ear. "Come on. Let's go inside."

Seth had set out a bottle of prosecco along with cheese and other nibbles before they went to the firepit. He poured flutes for both of them and toasted Evan.

"To us." Seth clinked their sensibly plastic barware together.

"To afterward." Evan tasted the wine on Seth's lips when they kissed.

It didn't take long to finish the first bottle as they made out on the couch in the living room. By unspoken agreement, they seemed to need being a little tipsy after the danger of the past few days.

"You're remarkably good about warming me up," Evan whispered. The gas fire lit up the darkened room and chased away the chill.

"I'm just getting started." Seth kissed his way up Evan's neck.

They had already shed their shirts, and by the time they were halfway through the second bottle, they were down to their briefs. Evan felt Seth's erection through the thin cotton rubbing against his equally enthusiastic cock.

"Bedroom." Evan stood and tugged Seth to come with him. Seth turned off the fireplace, checked the doors, and put a cork in the half-empty bottle. The nibbles were already gone.

"If you take too long, you're going to have to warm me up all over again." Evan fake-pouted as Seth let himself be pulled into the bedroom and laughed as Evan pounced on him, taking them both down on the mattress.

"Mine!" Evan starfished his body over Seth's to pin him.

"Always." Seth laughed, flipping them so he was on top and grinding against Evan's groin so there was no mistaking his intentions.

"What do you want?" Seth's voice was rough, and his eyes lust-blown.

"Everything. Anything. As long as we're together," Evan panted.

"These need to come off." Seth shoved Evan's briefs down and peeled off his own. Evan reached for the lube in the nightstand as Seth began to mouth and suck his way from throat to chest, stopping to pay plenty of attention to his nipples on the way to his abs and happy trail.

Seth shouldered between Evan's thighs, taking his cock down to the root in one move that left Evan gasping. Seth fondled Evan's balls, then teased his fingers farther back, skimming his taint to circle his hole.

"Yes. Please. Need you," Evan begged, running one hand through Seth's hair while the other clutched at the sheet.

Seth chuckled, and the low vibration resonated through Evan's already hard and leaking dick, making him shiver.

He grabbed the lube and slicked up his fingers, sliding first one and then two fingers into Evan, making sure to stroke the bundle of nerves that made Evan groan with pleasure.

"Don't make me wait," Evan panted. "Want to feel you."

Some nights, Seth enjoyed teasing Evan until he was aching for release. Tonight, both men seemed more focused on the comfort of joining than in acrobatics or endurance.

Seth popped his mouth off Evan's prick and drew himself up for a long, lingering kiss. "Roll over."

Evan obeyed, rising on his elbows and knees, legs parted, offering his ass.

Seth gripped Evan's hips and sank inside, going all the way to the hilt in one stroke, drawing moans from both.

"Move," Evan said, his voice muffled against the bedding.

"Toppy bottom," Seth teased, although they frequently switched. He obliged Evan's request, picking up his rhythm, not rough, but far from slow and easy.

"That's it...so good...please."

Seth wrapped his arms around Evan and sat back on his haunches, pulling Evan into his lap and giving himself full access to his lover's sensitive nipples and very hard cock.

"Oh God...yes," Evan moaned.

Seth shifted, hitting Evan's sweet spot, as he reached around and took Evan's stiff cock into his hand.

"I'm gonna...gonna..." Evan gasped.

"Let go," Seth whispered in his ear. "I've got you."

Evan shuddered with the strength of his orgasm, fountaining over Seth's hand. Seth came seconds later, deep inside Evan's tight channel.

Seth stroked Evan through the aftershocks until Evan slumped back against his shoulder, boneless and spent.

"You good?" Seth carefully folded forward to deposit Evan on the bed.

"Uh-huh." Evan sounded completely blissed out.

Seth kissed him and crossed the short distance to the bathroom, returning with a warm cloth to clean them, then washed up. He came back with the remainder of the prosecco.

"We should finish it. It'll go flat." Seth took a swig from the bottle.

"Classy," Evan joked in a warm, sated tone.

"Partying like rock stars," Seth teased back, handing off the wine to Evan.

They sat slumped against each other, propped against the headboard, passing the bottle back and forth until Seth laid the empty on the floor.

"That was...a great date night." Evan nestled against Seth's shoulder.

"Yeah?" Seth stroked his hand up and down Evan's arm.

Evan gave a sleepy nod.

"Then we'll have to do this kind of thing more often," Seth promised. "I like making you happy."

"I'll make you happy all over again in the morning." Evan gave Seth's groin a playful squeeze.

"That'll definitely give me sweet dreams." Seth pulled Evan close.

"Consider this practice for afterward," he said quietly. "When we're done, and we start over. Just you and me."

Evan smiled as he leaned up to kiss Seth. "Just us. Always."

AFTERWORD

The National Radio Quiet Zone is a real place, as are the restrictions on phones and wifi in the nearby area, especially around the Green Bank Observatory. I love finding a real location that lends itself to the story! The places I described in Pittsburgh on Seth and Evan's date night are also real, and if you're in the area, they make a great way to enjoy the city. The Trans-Allegheny Asylum and the Molly Stark Sanitorium are real as well and said to be extremely haunted.

Seth and Evan's epic adventure will continue, so stay tuned!

ACKNOWLEDGMENTS

Thank you so much to my editor, Jean Rabe, to my husband and writing partner, Larry N. Martin, for all his behind-the-scenes hard work, to my beta readers, and my wonderful cover artist Lou Harper. Thanks also to the Shadow Alliance and the Worlds of Morgan Brice reader street teams for their support and encouragement, plus my promotional crew and the ever-growing legion of ARC readers who help spread the word!

I couldn't do it without you! And, of course, thanks and love to my "convention gang" of fellow authors for making road trips and virtual cons fun.

ABOUT THE AUTHOR

Morgan Brice is the romance pen name of bestselling author Gail Z. Martin. Morgan writes urban fantasy male/male paranormal romance, with plenty of action, adventure, and supernatural thrills to go with the happily ever after.

Gail writes epic fantasy and urban fantasy, and together with co-author hubby Larry N. Martin, steampunk and comedic horror, all of which have less romance and more explosions.

On the rare occasions Morgan isn't writing, she's either reading, cooking, or spoiling two very pampered dogs.

Watch for additional new series from Morgan Brice and more books in the Witchbane, Badlands, Treasure Trail, Kings of the Mountain, Sharps & Springfield, and Fox Hollow universes coming soon!

Where to find me, and how to stay in touch

Join my Worlds of Morgan Brice Facebook Group and get in on all the behind-the-scenes fun! My free reader group is the first to see cover reveals, learn tidbits about works-in-progress, have fun with exclusive contests and giveaways, find out about in-person get-togethers, and more! It's also where I find my beta readers, ARC readers, and launch team! Come join the party! https://www.Facebook.com/groups/WorldsOfMorganBrice

Find me on the web at https://morganbrice.com. Sign up for my newsletter and never miss a new release! http://eepurl.com/dy_8oL. You can also find me on Twitter: @MorganBriceBook, on Pinterest (for Morgan and Gail): pinterest.com/Gzmartin, on Instagram as Morgan-BriceAuthor, on YouTube at https://www.youtube.com/c/GailZ-

MartinAuthor/ on Bookbub https://www.bookbub.com/authors/
morgan-brice and now on TikTok @MorganBriceAuthor

Check out the ongoing, online convention ConTinual www.face-book.com/groups/ConTinual

Support Indie Authors

When you support independent authors, you help influence what kind of books you'll see and what types of stories will be available because the authors themselves decide what to write, not a big publishing conglomerate. Independent authors are local creators supporting their families with the books they produce. Thank you for supporting independent authors and small press fiction!

ALSO BY MORGAN BRICE

Badlands Series

Badlands

Restless Nights, a Badlands Short Story

Lucky Town, a Badlands Novella

The Rising

Cover Me, a Badlands Short Story

Loose Ends

Night, a Badlands Short Story

Leap of Faith, a Badlands/Witchbane Novella

No Surrender

Point Blank

Fox Hollow Zodiac Series

Huntsman

Again

Fox Hollow Universe

Romp

Nutty for You

Imaginary Lover

Haven

Gruff

Kings of the Mountain Series

Kings of the Mountain

The Christmas Spirit, a Kings of the Mountain Short Story

Sins of the Fathers

Kings of the Mountain Universe

Roustabout

Sharps & Springfield Series

Peacemaker

Treasure Trail Series

Treasure Trail

Blink

Treasure Trail Universe

Light My Way Home, a Treasure Trail Novella

Witchbane Series

Witchbane

Burn, a Witchbane Novella

Dark Rivers

Flame and Ash

Unholy

The Devil You Know

Signs and Wonders

The Christmas Crunch, a Witchbane Short Story

Sandwiched, a Witchbane Short Story

Ambushed, a Witchbane Short Story